WRATH & RAIN BOOK THREE

VENGEFUL DEMON KING

NIKKI ST. CROWE

NIKKI ST. CROWE

Cover Design by TRC Designs by Cat

BEFORE YOU READ

Some of the content in this book may be triggering for some readers. If you'd like to learn more about trigger warnings in Nikki's work, please visit her website.

https://www.nikkistcrowe.com/content-warnings

CHAPTER
ONE

I'VE LOST TRACK OF THE NUMBER OF DAYS I'VE BEEN LOCKED IN THIS dungeon in the depths of the Demon King's castle.

For the first week, using a rock I'd found on the ground, I'd gouge a line in the slick black stone wall when the sun dipped below the horizon.

When I made it to day thirteen, I got so pissed, I threw the rock and now I can't find it.

Doesn't matter, I suppose.

Maybe Wrath will let me rot in this cell for an eternity.

Eternity.

My stomach suddenly wants to revolt, but it's damn near empty.

Wrath and I are connected. I was born of the *animus*, one third of the Demon King's power. If he can live forever, does that mean I will too?

Oh god.

I can't be trapped in this godforsaken hole forever.

My own sobs echo back to me when I curl into a ball in the corner and wrap my blanket around my shoulders.

Wrath came to me the first night I was in here and brought me this blanket.

It's the only time he's come.

There's a clank somewhere in the depths of the dungeon. I've come to recognize the sound of the main door being unbolted and opened and like Pavlov's dog, my stomach growls.

A few seconds later, I hear the distinct sound of Arthur's shoes shuffling over the gritty stone floor and then his face pops up in the cut-out in the wooden door of my cell.

I immediately smell food.

The dungeon might be old-fashioned, hollowed out from ancient stone, but someone took the time to install electricity down here and soft rope lights run the length of the hall along the floor. As Arthur unlocks my cell door and enters, the low lighting casts him in eerie shadows.

"Morning, Rain," he says.

"Good morning, Arthur." I make a show of stretching like I just woke up from the best night of sleep.

On my second day down here, Lauren was instructed to add metal cuffs to my wrists, much to her delight.

They look like iron bracelets etched with runes.

Now when I stretch, they thunk down the length of my arms and gouge skin as they do. Lauren wouldn't tell me what they were for, exactly, but I suspect it's just another measure to bind my power because when I've tried to use the *animus*, the runes glow and the cuffs burn.

"I have fresh clothes for you today," Arthur says. "And quiche."

My excitement is so acute, I damn near weep.

Arthur has been making sure I have clean clothes and a basin of soapy water every few days so I'm not a total feral beast in this dank cell.

And he seriously makes the best quiche.

"What kind? Quiche, that is." As if I'm going to be picky about it.

"Broccoli and ham."

I want to kiss the man.

Back slightly stooped, he comes over to me and hands off the tray. There's a permanent frown between his brows, and new lines of pain etched around his mouth.

"How are you, Arthur?"

"I'm okay." He stands back, clasps his hands.

"You don't look okay."

He's sheepish when he laughs. "The pain is worse today, is all. I overdid it yesterday."

I set the tray on the stone ledge by the window. "I thought Wrath was healing you?"

Arthur was in a bad car accident years ago and damaged his back. He has an electrical implant that's supposed to help with the chronic pain, but even that can only go so far.

Wrath's magic was helping him get by beyond what modern science could do.

"The Demon King doesn't have much power to spare these days," Arthur admits.

The guilt is immediate.

I helped Wrath's brother, Chaos, steal that power.

And because of it, Wrath is weak and Arthur is suffering.

"I'm so sorry, Arthur," I start. "I didn't—"

"No. No." Arthur holds up a hand. "The pain is mine and only mine. Please don't hold guilt over me."

I purse my lips and give him a nod.

"So beyond the power, how is he?" I ask.

Arthur casts his gaze to the floor and exhales, not quite a sigh, but almost. "The Demon King is…"

I lean forward, hanging on his hesitation, hungrier for the details about Wrath than I am for the actual food.

The truth is, I'm starving for him in a way that makes me want to claw out of my skin. I'm restless for him.

I didn't think it was possible to want to love and murder someone all at the same time, but the Demon King has proven me wrong.

He tried to force my hand, make me bind myself to him, and when I refused, he hurt my best friend.

I'll never forgive him for it.

But I don't know how else to punish him either. We are linked because of the *animus*, or rather, because I *am* the *animus* —the Hellfire Crown, one third of the Demon King's power.

If he bleeds, so do I, and vice versa.

I can't punish him physically without physically wounding myself too.

But something tells me the bruises I've left on him are not the kind you can see.

"The Demon King is what? Tell me, Arthur." My voice is quiet and desperate and the echo of it fills the hollowed-out crevices of the cell like a ghost.

"I've never seen him like this," Arthur admits.

"Like what?"

When he finally looks at me, there's worry pinched in the aged lines around his eyes. "Broken."

It's a punch to the gut. A knife to the chest.

I did that.

I did that.

He made me do it.

He gave me no choice.

My frustration burbles up, barbed and burning, and the magical cuffs around my wrists glow bright red.

The metal heats up, runes etched into it glowing brightly.

Then the metal singes my skin as a snap of electricity jolts down to bone.

I yell out and fight at the cuffs like I always do, like this time will be any different from the two dozen other times I tried to use my magic. Like this time maybe they'll come off.

They don't.

The pain reverberates through me and settles at my breastbone. It's a deep ache that will last an hour or so, if I could tell time down here.

Arthur frowns at me.

I shake out my arms, then press my hand to my sternum as if I can massage away the pain. "And Chaos? Dare I even ask?"

"Chaos has been busy."

I curse into the shadows. "What kind of busy?"

"He seems to be working with Naomi now."

"The president is working with the Demon King's brother?"

Arthur nods. "You know the saying. 'The enemy of my enemy—'"

"'Is my friend,'" I finish.

"Precisely."

"Great." I pace the length of the cell. It takes me all of two seconds. "What about the state of the world?"

"Oddly enough," Arthur says, "things have quieted down. We haven't had a mass shooting in over three weeks. A new record since they started recording those stats. And the political unrest has seemed to settle too."

This should be good news. So why does it feel like a shoe about to drop?

"Does Wrath have a theory as to why things have settled?"

"Chaos can bring order just the same as he can cause chaos. He and Wrath are two sides of the same coin, in a way. They represent both."

"So Chaos is what, giving us some zen magic?"

"I guess you could say that."

"Until he decides to flip the switch."

I don't know enough about Wrath's brother to know what his plan is. Maybe Wrath doesn't know either. But it would be in Chaos's best interest to have our government on his side while he fights his brother, and how else could he prove his value than through the tempering of our country's unrest?

It makes Wrath look like a hurricane in comparison.

"Has he...Wrath...has he said anything about me?"

I hate how desperate I sound, but I wouldn't ask anyone other than Arthur. I know he won't judge me.

Arthur frowns. "No, I'm sorry."

I exhale, shoulders dipping. "It's okay. I mean, that's what I expected but if he had plans to murder me, I just wanted a heads up."

"He won't," Arthur says maybe too quickly. "Whatever he means to do with you, it won't be that."

"Because he can't," I point out. "I'm sure he wishes he could."

"I'm not going to pretend to understand what goes on inside the Demon King's head," Arthur admits, "but one thing I do know? He has no weakness but you."

There's a sharp sting in my eyes that feels an awful lot like tears.

I want to go to him. I wish he would let me. We could torture each other, scream at each other, then fuck each other until we were spent.

The reality of our relationship feels like a chain around my ankle, one I'll never escape.

I should embrace it. Stop fighting it. I just wish he wasn't so much of...

A villain.

"Do you think he'll ever let me out of this hole?" I ask Arthur.

"I don't know, Rain."

I nod and collapse against the back wall. "Thank you for the food. You're the bright spot of my day, Arthur."

He smiles a closed-lip smile. "I wish I could do more."

"I know."

He ambles over to the door, grabs my empty tray from yesterday, and then clanks open the lock with his key.

I think it says something that Wrath sends Arthur to attend to me when I could so easily overpower him, especially now that he's suffering from constant pain again.

The Demon King knows I won't fight Arthur—I've got too much of a soft heart. And I think he knows deep down that I won't run. I can't. There's nowhere to run to.

Arthur gets the bolt open and then slips out of the cell. The lock clanks again as he shuts it. "I'll see you tomorrow."

I go to the tray of food and eat it standing at the window ledge. Looking through the old bubbled glass is like looking through a dream. The world outside is hazy and swirled, but the dark shape at the edge of the garden is distinct, nonetheless.

The Demon King is stalking through the garden from the house to the stables, if I had to guess.

It's the first time I've caught sight of him since he ordered Lauren to drag me down to this hole and my heart thuds loudly in my chest reminding me that even when I want to hate him, I don't.

I'm suddenly buzzing.

I drop my fork and wrap my hands around the iron bars inlaid in the windowsill as if I can get closer and get a better look. He's in profile to me and I can just make out the hard line of his mouth and the tension in his shoulders.

Look at me.

Look at me.

I'm so desperate for his gaze that a choked cry escapes my throat.

The Demon King stops.

His body goes rigid, hands balling into fists.

He looks my way, to the window to my cell.

Can he see me through the glass? Can he hear me?

The scowl that comes over his face is sharp enough to cut.

I think my heart stops beating for several seconds as we stare at each other across the expanse of the garden, through the thick, swirled glass.

He is not a dream.

The Demon King is a nightmare come to life.

His eyes burn bright red for a half second before he turns away from me and disappears from sight.

CHAPTER
TWO

EVEN THOUGH I WAS BORN WITH STUBBORNNESS STITCHED INTO EVERY fiber of my being, going on a hunger strike is absolutely out of the question.

For one, I like food.

And two, Arthur is a damn good cook.

I eat the entire slice of quiche and then mop up the crust crumbs with the tip of my index finger. If I was a free woman, I'd be going for seconds, damn the calories and the thick hips.

I set the tray at the door and then begin my nightly ritual of absolutely fucking nothing.

I pace for a while. Then do some push-ups which I suck at. Then I play this other game I invented called Reach for the Rock.

There's a sharp, black stone just out of my reach in the hallway outside the cell. I spotted it after I threw my first rock and lost it. But no matter how far I reach, I can never put my fingers to it.

It keeps me busy though.

Sometime later, sweating and angry—I want that fucking rock—I grab my blanket and wedge myself into the back corner of the stone cell. There's this semi-comfortable spot where the stone dips in a way that is the perfect cup for my back.

Ahh, it's the little things, right?

I'm going to go insane down here.

I doze sitting up.

I don't know how long or what time it is when I wake.

But I'm sure that I'm not alone.

There's only the glow of the inset lights outside my cell, but I can make out the void of a dark shape in the far corner of my prison.

"Are you really here?" I ask him.

"Does it matter?"

The sound of his voice is like a drag of silk over my skin and I'm immediately shivering in my blanket.

"I think it would," I say.

There's the glint of something in his hand and at first, I think it's a blade, but then I realize it's a glass. He takes a sip. I hear the distinct sound of ice clinking together in the dark.

"Then yes," he says, "I am really here."

His speech is slow and slurred.

"Are you drunk?"

"Very much so," he admits.

"I didn't think you could get drunk."

"I had to go to considerable effort to manage it." He takes another long drink and then comes forward. The shadows writhe around him like living things. He sets the glass on the window ledge and takes another step, but he's unsteady on his feet.

Hugging the blanket to my shoulders, I rise to stand in the corner unsure of where this is going, afraid of where it could, excited that it might go somewhere, anywhere at all.

I am a glutton for punishment. That's never truer than when I'm in the same room as the Demon King.

Maybe I'm going to hell for all of this. If there *is* a hell.

Maybe I'm already there.

I want to sink into the fire. Feel the heat of it, *of him*, on my skin.

"What do you want?" I ask him.

"I want you to obey me."

I snort. The sound echoes in the cavern. "I won't. Not ever. But I think you know that."

He collapses against the wall. "I suppose I do."

"So what do you really want?"

He bows his head. His chest rises and falls. He says nothing for the longest time and my heart hammers at my eardrums.

Thud. Thud. Thud.

"I want to know what to do with you."

My stomach fills with butterflies.

I think this might be the most telling thing that's ever come out of his mouth.

What he really wants to do is force me to do as he wishes—bind myself to him, bow at his feet, obey him—but he can't.

Wrath is a king and no one has ever defied him, and yet the power he holds over me is scant, barely power at all.

"Why did you hurt Gus?"

He comes closer and steps out of the shadows.

In so many days, I somehow forgot what it was to look him straight in the face.

As soon as his pale beauty is in front of me, the air catches in my throat and I have to gulp it back.

"I've never had the luxury of being merciful," he admits.

"Gus is my best friend."

His gaze finds me in the dim light. "And I've never had the luxury of a friend."

"I was your friend."

"No, you weren't."

"Yes, I was!" My voice rises and bounces off the stone. "I wanted you. I wanted this." I wave my hand between us. "I wanted it all."

"Tell me, how does it taste when those lies roll off your tongue? Sweet like honey? Bitter like anise? Or maybe they taste like nothing at all. Maybe you are immune to them entirely."

"Don't do that."

"Do what?"

"Don't pretend that I'm the bad guy here. I was willing to do whatever it took to help you and—"

He looks down at me, down the sharp slope of his nose. "Everything except for the one thing I fucking needed."

"You wanted me to bind myself to you forever. And you didn't even give me the time to consider what that meant."

"We didn't *have* time, Rain."

Him using my real name is like a slap to the face and I shrink back from it.

He always calls me *dieva*.

I thought it meant little girl, but it's actually more like a promise, a promise to protect that which he's claimed.

It became a term of endearment. And the loss of it is the same as being gutted.

Tears immediately well in my eyes and I wish I could use my newfound power to blip out of sight.

I don't want Wrath to know he can get to me with something so easy as calling me by my name.

"It wasn't a killing blow," he says, low and beneath his breath.

"What?"

He meets my gaze again and the first hint of red fire is flaring in his irises. "I've spilled enough blood in my lifetime to know how to spill only what I need. Your friend wasn't in any danger. Not really."

For some reason this makes me even angrier. "So you did it just to scare me into doing what you wanted."

"That's precisely what it was."

"You're an asshole."

He crosses the distance between us, his face morphing into the monster. "No, I am a king!" His voice booms through the cell and echoes down the hall. "I do what I must! And you're just a stupid little girl who sacrifices so little to have so much."

My own rage burbles up my throat.

Fuck him and fuck his arrogance.

Without thinking, I grab his abandoned glass from the windowsill and smash it against the stone wall. I'm left with a long, pointy shard in my hand.

He looks at it, then looks at me, his mouth twitching.

Staring him right in the fucking face, I drag the sharp end of the glass over the pale underside of my arm.

The pain is acute. White dots burst in my field of vision and I grit my teeth against it as my skin splits open and blood wells out.

Wrath's eyes narrow to slits as his jaw flexes.

It may be dark in the cell, but even in what little light there is, I can see the mirroring wound on his arm, his blood dripping to the stone floor and pooling in the divots.

When I bleed, he bleeds.

"Maybe I'll just slit my throat so I can finally be done with you," I say.

"You're too fucking stubborn."

I bring the shard to my neck.

His eyes pinch tighter, his chest rising with a quick breath and then absolute stillness as he holds it in.

I'm not sure if I'm bluffing. Or if I'm tempting the connection between us and the power of the dark father god burning through my veins.

Can I die?

I'm the *animus*, one third of the legendary dark god's power. Maybe there's no such thing as death for me.

But I like seeing the mighty Demon King flinch.

Grip tight on the shard, it cuts into the palm of my hand and across the meaty parts of my fingers. I'm a mess. Blood is already pouring down my hand, down my arm, dripping from my elbow.

I move to pull the glass over my throat.

The Demon King snaps his hand out and grips me at the wrist, stopping me.

"Don't," he says.

There is the barest flicker of panic in his voice.

I don't know if it's for me or for him. Or maybe both. Maybe it's impossible to unsnarl us now.

"Let me out of this fucking hole."

He takes another breath, but his grip remains on my wrist, fingers circling me like a vise.

"Why did you refuse me?" He gets in close, overwhelming me with his size and the sheer power of his body. "I would have protected you."

A sob threatens to escape from my throat, so I clamp my teeth, trying to catch it before it does.

The most painful thing is, I believe him.

I think if I'd agreed to bind myself to him, he would have kept his promises. I would have had him in my bed every night. I would have had his dark power at my side. I would have ruled on a throne beside him if I'd wanted.

Every man and woman and demon and vampire would have bowed at my feet, jealous of what I had and they didn't.

"Why did you refuse me?" he asks again. "Tell me."

I have nothing to hide. And even though I hate the idea of him thinking of me like *a stupid little girl*, I want him to trust that what comes out of my mouth is always the truth, despite what he may think.

"Because I was afraid, just like you said."

He runs his knuckles down the side of my face, a featherlight touch, but he leaves a trail of blood on my skin. It's hot at first and cools quickly in the dank air of the cell.

"And now?" he asks.

"Now I'm terrified."

"Do you want to know a secret?" he whispers.

"Yes."

"So am I." He pulls my hand away and wrenches the glass from my grip. It plinks into the shadows when he tosses it aside. "I'm terrified of being weak," he admits. "And I'm terrified of how I feel whenever you're not by my side."

I shiver as his hand comes to my throat. "And how's that? How does it make you feel?"

"Like I've been cleaved in two." He tightens his hold, fingers punishing me for making him feel the way he does.

I've laid him low.

The mighty Demon King.

When I walk out of this cell, I will be ten feet tall.

I grab hold of his hair with my bloody hand and yank him to me. Our mouths collide. He bites at my bottom lip, drawing blood and hissing when an answering wound must come to his mouth.

I taste the coppery tang of our blood.

He wraps his arms around me and lifts me up, pressing me against the stone wall as he tears the shirt from my body.

The material rips loudly in the chamber and the sound tangles with the echo of our pants, our groans.

We are famished for something that cannot be bought.

His mouth comes to my neck, his sharp teeth dragging over my sensitive flesh. I moan and instinctively curl away from the pain, but he is relentless. He nips at me again and I jolt beneath him, rocking against his crotch.

There is a considerable bulge there.

Grabbing the center of my bra, he rips the material from my body, exposing me to the chill air. More blood drips from his mouth which covers me in splatters as he hoists me up, capturing my nipple in the heat of his mouth.

His tongue slides over me, drawing me to a peak and the pulse of the pleasure scorches down my belly and sinks into my clit.

The Demon King might not know what to do with me outside of this cell, but he sure as hell knows what to do with me now.

Anchoring me to the wall, he rolls my other nipple between his fingers, sending a shot of pain and pleasure through my nerves.

I cry out in the dark.

I want him inside of me.

Right fucking now.

I squirm beneath him, trying to get my hand between us so I can pull him out of his pants.

I manage to snag the waistband and yank them down and his cock hangs heavy and thick between us.

When I take him in my fist, his eyes slip closed as his Adam's apple sinks on a deep, guttural groan.

"I've missed that hand on my cock," he says.

"You knew where to find me."

"I was punishing you."

"Sounds like you were only punishing yourself."

He drops me, grabs a fistful of my hair and forces me to my knees.

"I missed fucking that disobedient mouth even more."

He shoves inside of me. He's so fucking hard and when he

thrusts forward, the head of his dick hits the back of my throat and I gag.

He tsk-tsks above me. "Be a good girl and take it," he says and thrusts in again causing my belly to burn bright with a deep-rooted, so fucked-up sense of pride.

He fucks me hard and fast, his hand still tangled in my hair, guiding me over his length.

"Fuck," he says. "You will be the end of me."

Precum fills my mouth and he slows his pace, straining to hold back.

"Get up," he orders and strips me of the rest of my clothes as his eyes burn bright red in the dark.

I can feel the wetness coating me, slipping down my thighs. My clit is swollen and needy.

The *norrow* appear beside me.

"What are—"

The dark shadowmen grab me, flip me around and slam me to the floor. I huff out a breath and dirt crusts in my mouth. Wrath kicks my legs apart and sinks between them.

I flail beneath the norrow, but their hold is steady and a seed of panic blooms in my chest as my heart slams in my ears.

Wrath's fingers slip beneath my mound, hitting my clit. I pant against the floor, filled with a too-big feeling, like I might burst open at the seams.

"Wrath," I moan. "Please."

He slips two fingers inside of me, slides a third forward against my swollen bud.

A flare of pleasure burns at my core.

"Fuck." I'm trying so hard to catch my breath. "Fuck me."

His fingers disappear and he cracks me across the ass. The pain is immediate and catches me off guard and I can't help but yelp in the dark.

"Beg for it."

I groan. He cups me between the legs and I squirm, mindless and buzzing trying to burn friction between us, to feel the edge of pleasure.

It's too much. It's too much. It's all too much and not enough.

Blood is crusting on my arm and down my chest. Dirt grits on my open wound.

I can feel the primordial shiver of the norrow on my skin, like a dark daydream.

I am mindless and found all at the same time.

Found by Wrath, the dark Demon King.

"Please." The buzz between my legs is a flame I need stoked. Right fucking now. "Please fuck me."

He grabs me by the hips and yanks my ass up, baring me more.

When the head of his cock comes to my opening, I almost weep with relief.

A breath stutters out of me.

The norrow disappear.

Wrath rocks back and drives into me, seating himself to the hilt.

Pain blooms at my core, he's so deep.

He fucks me hard and the sound of our primal fucking echoes through the cavern.

The pleasure builds.

And builds.

Wrath groans as he pounds into me.

His dark magic writhes around the cavern floor, then pulls in tight, and when I feel the diving caress of it at my clit, I almost lose my mind.

"Come for me, *dieva*," Wrath says. "Call out my name."

"Wrath," I say on a moan.

"No," he scolds, his grip tightening on my hips. "Try again."

The darkness writhes around my pussy, teases at my clit, coaxing the pleasure from my well. It's a divine swirl, a featherlight touch with just the right rhythm to drive me wild.

Fuck. I'm a quivering, wet mess.

"Go on," he says, punishing me by slowing his thrusts. In and out. In and out.

The cuffs on my wrists light up and the metal grows hot as the orgasm reaches out for me.

"Fuck. Oh fuck. Wrath."

He takes another fistful of my hair and wrenches me back. The growl of his anger rumbles in my ear. "Say it, *dieva*."

"My king," I correct.

"Good girl," he says and thrusts deeper.

The darkness circles my clit with a divine rhythm and the wave crests, then spills over, burning through my veins, all of the muscle in my body tensing up.

Wrath drives deep and comes with a deep, guttural groan, the sound echoing around us in the stone cell.

He pulls back, sinks in again, the head of his cock swelling inside of me, hitting deep at the center.

I tremble through the aftershock of the orgasm, racing like an electrical current through my veins.

When we've both ridden the wave out, we collapse on the dirt floor on our backs.

We both pant into the dark.

Where the fuck do we go from here?

He might have controlled that descent into dark pleasure, but we both know he's as mad for me as I am for him.

We are the thorns in each other's side and every time we try to pluck the other out, the thorn sinks deeper.

"Let me out of this fucking hole," I say.

"I like knowing exactly where I can find you."

I lift my arms and the metal cuffs sink down my wrists. "You've literally handcuffed me."

"I know. I like that too."

I groan into the dark.

"At least let me have a shower."

"So you can clean my cum from your pussy?"

"Wrath."

He rolls to his knees, then scoops me up effortlessly.

One second, we're in the dankness of the dungeon and the next we're in the warm hush of his bedroom.

I almost weep.

But I'm not going to let him know how badly I wanted out of that prison. I'm just going to pretend that it was a mild annoyance, a slight inconvenience.

He promised to torture me and any sign of discomfort would be a mark on his side.

I will not let him win.

I keep my arms locked around his neck as he carries me into the bathroom and sets me down on the black stone floor of the walk-in shower.

Only the undercabinet lighting is on, so it's easy on my eyes considering I've spent the last two weeks in almost total darkness.

He reaches around me and flips on the showerhead, dials in the temperature.

I try not to like that he's taking care of me. Of course I fail at that.

I wanted to believe that I was just an innocent bystander yanked into Wrath's darkness, but the truth is, whatever it is we have here makes me euphoric in all of its dark, fucked-up glory.

Turns out living on a knife's edge is exhilarating.

And being cared for by the infamous Demon King is like holding the flame of a god in your hand.

It'll surely burn you, but the thrill of holding it is so fucking worth it.

When steam fills the stall, I walk in beneath the water and a moan escapes me.

"You have ten minutes," he says.

"Yes, warden."

He growls before disappearing in a whirl of black magic.

CHAPTER
THREE

When I'm showered and wrapped in a towel, I come out to Wrath's bedroom. There's a bedside lamp on, but Wrath is nowhere to be found.

I tiptoe around the room and put my ear to the door. I don't hear anything beyond it. I go to the balcony next and pull open the French doors. Wrath's bedroom is on the second floor and the balcony overlooks the back garden.

I'm sure I could scale down the railing and hop down to the ground and run away through the woods.

But running seems futile now.

And besides, I'm naked again with no clothes. Why the hell do I keep finding myself in this predicament?

"Thinking of trying to escape already?"

His voice finds me on the balcony and a shiver runs down my spine. I turn to him and clutch at the towel.

I'm not a liar—most of the time—so I dodge the question entirely like the artful little scamp I am. "It feels like it's been months since I breathed fresh air."

He rolls his eyes. "It's been two weeks and no more. So dramatic. Get inside, *dieva*."

There's a satisfied thrill low in my gut hearing him use my pet name.

It feels like I'm standing on solid ground again.

I come inside. He disappears and pops up beside me a half second later. He wraps his hand around the back of my neck and steers me over to the bed where I notice there's a chain screwed into the headboard.

"I didn't know we were going full BDSM," I say as he tosses me on the bed, grabs one of my arms and clamps the chain to the cuff around my wrist. "Is this really necessary?"

He gives me a sardonic smile. "You've run from me twice, betrayed me multiple times, stabbed me, and summoned my brother only for him to take one third of the triad, putting us both at risk. So yes, it's absolutely necessary. Unless you'd like to return to the hole?"

"No," I say, a bit too quickly, then twist my mouth into a salacious smile. "Chained to your bed is fine by me."

He snorts and turns away.

"Where are you going?"

"I have work to do, *dieva*." He glares at me over his shoulder. "And a mess to clean up."

Then he's gone.

"You could have at least offered me a drink!" I yell.

He doesn't respond, so I just lay in his bed, naked and chained, and a little miffed. I mean, this is definitely a step up from a stone floor. Wrath's bed feels like laying in a cloud. And it's definitely a lot warmer than the dungeon. But the cuffs and the chain are chafing and frankly, really fucking annoying.

I test the chain by giving it a few hard yanks, but of course the Demon King is no slouch. The damn thing is screwed in tight.

I drop against the pillows, forcing air out of the fluff and I'm immediately surrounded by his scent.

Now I'm soaring. Wrath's scent might be a fucking drug and I think I might be an addict.

It's like wintertime beneath the stars, a crackling fire, and something spicy in a hot mug between your hands.

I take a deep inhale, filling my nose and my lungs with it.

I could huff this fume all day. Begrudgingly, of course.

Trying to find a comfortable spot, what with being chained to the bed, I curl onto my side and tuck my arm beneath the pillow. The stuffing is just thick enough to soften some of the sharp edges of the chain and cuff.

I breathe out.

From this moment on, I will never take a comfortable bed for granted.

I'm realizing that the *animus* might have shielded me from physical ailments my entire life. I never gave it a second thought, but looking back, I wasn't ever sick. What few scrapes and bumps and bruises I suffered were gone within a day.

But sleeping on a stone floor for a week? The dark god's power can only do so much.

I decide I'll just lie there in Wrath's bed for a while and rest my aching bones before I start strategizing my next move, but before I know it, I'm fast asleep.

And it isn't until hours later that I feel the bed dip beneath the Demon King's weight, the warmth of his chest at my back and his arms around my body.

I'm barely awake, but I swear, even through the sleepy fog, I hear him sigh into my neck.

Almost like he's relieved to have me by his side.

CHAPTER
FOUR

WHEN I WAKE IN THE DAYLIGHT, THE DEMON KING IS GONE AGAIN. But I'm still chained to the bed.

Annoyance flashes through me. I feel the now familiar sensation of my power lighting up, but the force of it is quickly snuffed out by the magical cuffs around my wrist.

"Goddammit," I mutter. Then, "Wrath! Hello!"

Because I'm the world's luckiest girl, it's Lauren that responds to my shouting.

Rolling my eyes, I lie back against the pillows, tugging the blanket around me.

"Naked in the Demon King's bed again," she says. "Why am I not surprised?"

"Yes, yes. I know. Get it out. Go ahead. The slut is bending over for him. Blah blah blah. Can I please have some clothes?"

She yanks the drapes open and sunlight pours into the room, burning my eyes. Groaning, I throw an arm over my face.

"I'm not sure if I have any more clothing to spare. You keep finding yourself without yours. I'm running out."

"I'll owe you."

She blows out a breath. "As if you have anything to give me."

"Can I be unchained?"

"I don't have the key."

"Of course you don't. Where is Wrath?"

"The Demon King is currently in Saint Sabine meeting with Kat."

"Why?"

"If he wanted you to know why, he would have told you, I'm sure."

Being chained to this bed is punishment enough—now I have to be forced to endure Lauren's snark.

I don't think she'll ever warm up to me and her bad attitude has me constantly questioning why Wrath keeps her around.

If I were a vindictive asshole, I'd be scheming to get rid of her.

Do I have that power with the Demon King?

There's a snarly little flare of pride that tells me maybe I do.

"For the love of all things holy," I beg, "can I please have some clothes?"

She rolls her eyes, lets out a long grumbly sigh, and leaves the room.

I test out the chain again and don't get it to budge. It'll be much easier to investigate once I'm dressed.

Lauren returns with a tangled ball of clothing and dumps it on the end of the bed. "There you go, princess," she says and leaves again.

"Hey! I can't reach them!"

But of course, she's not here to make things easier for me.

I spend the next fifteen minutes stretched out on the bed like a man about to be quartered and hung. I manage to grab the clothing with my toes and yank it up the massive length of the bed.

The panties and shorts are easy to put on, though it takes some shimmying around. I get the bra on—thank god it's a hook closure—but have to leave one of the straps off for the chain.

"Now we're in business." I stand on the bed and kick the pillows aside. Using all of my strength, I wrap both arms around the chain and yank.

My teeth grit together. Sweat beads on my forehead.

I blow out a breath. "Okay, new strategy."

I prop a foot on the headboard and use my leg for leverage. When that doesn't work, I pull the chain taut and brace both feet on the headboard like I'm a climber rappelling down a mountainside.

"Come...on...god...dammit!"

Nothing.

Doesn't even budge.

I fall back to the bed, sweaty and spent.

"A spirited effort," the Demon King says.

I wince and bury a grumble. "It's unbecoming to watch a girl struggle from the shadows."

"Here, let me help you."

The darkness kicks up around me. Inky tendrils trail up my legs, up my thighs, and a shiver courses up my body.

The dark ribbons steal beneath the hem of my shorts and the anticipation of their destination makes my heart thud loudly in my head, and a tingle buzz in my clit.

"Wrath." I pull myself up against the mountain of pillows.

The Demon King drops into one of the wingback chairs in the shadows.

"What did I promise you, *dieva*?"

The darkness slips around the hem of my panties and cups me, pulsing against me.

"Fuck you."

"What did I promise you?"

"That my suffering has only begun."

"Yes."

The darkness pulls in closely, a whisper against my clit.

I sink back against the pillows and close my eyes.

This doesn't feel like suffering and the fear that it could flip at any moment somehow makes the pleasure that much more potent.

The ribbons of darkness rock against me, swirling and teasing at my bud.

I'm wet in an instant and the darkness pools together to a swollen head, sinking to my opening.

I hear the shift of fabric as the Demon King rises from his chair.

"As a king," he says, "I've learned there are different kinds of suffering."

The darkness pushes inside of me, filling me up, and fucks me slow and steady.

The chain rattles as I writhe on the bed and I wrap my arm around it, as if to anchor me there.

"There is the suffering of pain."

A ribbon winds up across my torso, steals inside my bra and caresses my nipple.

"There is the suffering of want."

The pace of the darkness picks up, driving into me over and over. My pleasure builds, my breathing quickening.

The crest is rising, rising.

"Oh fuck, keep going."

I spread my legs further apart letting the darkness take me.

I'm so close.

The pressure builds.

And then—

Gone.

"And there is the suffering of loss."

"Wait. Wrath, please—"

I writhe on the bed and yank at the chain.

"Wrath."

He's at the bedside now, peering down at me, the sunlight limning him in silver, his face hidden in shadow.

The orgasm is haunting me like a ghost, so fucking close, just out of reach.

I'm still buzzing.

It would take just the slightest bit of friction and I'd be spilling over the edge again.

Wrath climbs on the bed and my inner walls clench, anticipating the feel of his cock inside of me.

Kneeling between my legs, he scoops me up and sets me on his lap. I can tell he's hard through his pants and the bulge rocks against my hot center.

The chain grows taut.

"I think I've suffered enough," I say with a ragged breath.

"No, you haven't." His mouth is close to mine. He has the softest lips and the most punishing of kisses.

I lock my legs around him and grind over his cock.

"Fuck me."

He leans forward, presses his lips against mine, lets me taste the sweetness of his tongue.

I moan into his mouth. He's going to give in to me. I know he will. If I just keep him here and—

Suddenly, I'm weightless and falling back. I yelp and collapse against the bed.

Wrath disappeared.

Fucking hell.

I scurry back into a sitting position and find him at the end

29

of the bed, leaning against the bed post. He's watching me with hooded eyes and a satisfied smile on his face.

"Asshole," I say. "As usual, a girl only has herself to count on. I guess I'll just finish myself."

I'm baiting him, but he doesn't bite.

I slip my hand down the flat plane of my stomach and then beneath the waistband of my shorts and into my panties.

I'm so fucking wet, my fingers are immediately slippery and when I slide them over myself, the sensation is exquisite.

I rest my head against the headboard and close my eyes.

I go slowly at first, tempting him.

My clit begs for more as the pressure builds, but I want to drag this out. I want to punish him as much as he's punishing me.

Wanting more lubrication, I dip a finger into my slick channel and then drag my finger back up, drenching the rest of me.

When I open my eyes and look over at Wrath, his irises are glowing molten red.

I love getting beneath his skin.

I slip my hand out, bring my fingers to my mouth and suck each fingertip clean with the roll of my tongue.

He growls.

I sink back to my clit and pick up the tempo, turning quick circles with the pads of my fingers.

Fuck. Fuck I'm close.

I like him watching me.

My breathing quickens, chest rising and falling with the building orgasm as my body tenses up, ready for the pleasure to burst through.

"Oh fuck," I moan.

There is a moment when I'm about to spill over the edge that I think he'll stop me, and the anticipation of the pleasure being stolen from me makes the actual orgasm slam through me like a bright flame.

I cry out. The chain rattles as my body tenses up. My thighs rub together, muscle and bone quivering as the pleasure rides through me.

I jerk and the chain goes taut again, then bangs against the headboard when I fold into myself.

The bed sinks as the Demon King comes up between my legs and forces my knees open.

My hand is still curled over my mound. Just the slightest movement might send me over the edge again.

"Give me your hand," he tells me.

I breathe out quickly, trembling beneath him.

"*Dieva*," he scolds.

I pull my hand from my clit, from my panties. My fingers glisten in the light.

Wrath wraps his hand around my wrist and brings me to his mouth. He sucks one finger in, drags his tongue over my fingertip, cleaning off my juices.

He moves to the next finger and cleans that one too.

The feel of his tongue is a sensation I wasn't prepared for and butterflies ignite in my belly.

This is the hottest fucking thing I've ever seen him do.

I'm quivering again, full of a sensation I can't name.

When he's finished, he holds my hand up. "It's as I suspected," he says.

"What?"

"I can still taste my cum in your pussy. From now on, I want your pussy to always be dripping with it." He bends over me and the hard ridge of his cock presses into me. "I want every vampire, demon, and shifter within a ten-mile radius to know who you belong to."

The darkness pulls in around us, blotting out the sunlight as Wrath wraps his hand around my throat.

"Then why didn't you fill me up again, huh? Why deny me?"

His jaw clenches, teeth gritting.

"Why, Wrath?"

"Because I can't spend every waking minute buried in your pussy."

"It doesn't sound so bad to me."

"You had your chance."

"You mean if I bound myself to you, I'd have you in my bed?"

"I would have given you the world," he admits and then flinches as if he didn't mean to say it out loud.

"The world for my obedience."

He narrows his eyes.

"There are thousands who would give anything to be where you are."

"Full of the Demon King's cum?" I give the chain a hard yank. "Chained to his bed?"

His teeth grind together.

"You know what's hilarious about that?" I counter. "They would have bowed to you, but this power that burns through my veins? They never would have been strong enough to contain it. I don't bow to you because I don't have to. Because I am not your inferior. Start treating me like your equal and maybe we can come to an agreement."

"You are not equal to me."

I snort and roll my eyes. "Tell that to the *animus*. Go on, she's listening."

He growls and climbs off of me as the darkness pulls back and the sunlight fills the room again.

The tension of the moment is gone.

He unlocks me from the chain, but the magical cuffs stay on my wrists.

He lingers, bent over me. The air grows charged, electric.

His hand comes up as if he means to push aside a lock of my hair, but at the last second, he shifts and gives one of my magical cuffs a tug to test its strength.

I'm left aching.

"Come downstairs when you're ready," he says and then pulls away.

"You're going to leave me here alone, unchained? Maybe I'll tie a rope out of your silky sheets and scale down the balcony like a girl trapped in a dark fairytale."

He levels me with an annoyed scowl. "I wonder...if I drown you in a shallow pool, will I survive? No blood will be drawn." His gaze goes distant as he considers it. "I'm certainly willing to experiment."

I grumble. "I'll be down in ten minutes."

"Good girl," he says and disappears.

Truth be told, I wasn't planning on running. I just like to rile him up.

If I pretend I hate his guts, then I don't have to face the inconceivable truth—that I don't.

I take my time in the bathroom and comb out my hair with a spare brush I find in one of the drawers. It's been forever since I felt put together and presentable. Not that it should matter, considering I'm a prisoner here.

Now that I'm unchained, I can finish dressing. I grab the t-shirt Lauren found me and hold it up.

"Fuck me."

It literally says DEMON SLUT across the chest.

I've seen these shirts hanging in the windows of the goth shop in the strip mall outside of Norton Harbor. They're Demon King licensed merch, though I don't know who holds the license. Certainly not the Demon King himself. This kind of tomfoolery is beneath him, as my mom loves to say.

Lauren planned this. I have to give her a gold star for patience and ingenuity.

I put the shirt on and make my way downstairs and to the Bourbon Room. Wrath is there with Arthur and Lauren.

When she sees me in my slutty shirt, a smirk spreads across her lip-glossed lips.

Wrath takes one look at me, his eyes dragging over the big block letters covering my chest and a scowl deepens the sharp lines of his face.

He turns that scathing look on Lauren and she braces.

It's a goddamn delight.

There's something I'm learning about Lauren—she's not very bright.

She's so desperate to make me look bad and to have the Demon King's attention that she never stops to actually strategize about the proper way of making that happen.

I almost feel sorry for her.

Her dumb devotion to him is going to get her head lopped off one of these days.

Though I hope that's just figurative and not literal.

I might dislike her, but I don't dislike her that much.

There's a moment where I think Wrath might punish her now, but apparently her cowering satisfies him, because he moves on without calling her out.

Damn.

"Arthur," he says, "why don't you bring our traitor up to speed and show her the news conference from yesterday."

"Will that be my new nickname?" I ask lightly. "It's much easier to pronounce than *dieva*."

He walks over to the bar. "I do like the ring of it."

Arthur busies himself with the TV remote and tries to pretend we're not all at each other's throats. Poor Arthur.

He clicks on the screen and brings up a news conference at the White House podium. Naomi Wright is there and Chaos is by her side.

I cross my arms over my Demon Slut t-shirt while the footage plays.

"Our country has been subjected to far too much carnage." Naomi looks across the assembled press, but then shifts to the camera, to the viewer. She's dressed in her usual blazer, the pearls in her ears and around her neck. I wanted to hate the president for what happened to me in Riverside Park when her soldiers turned on me, but maybe she was in the exact same position I was just a week ago, feeling like she was stuck between two opposing forces with no easy way out.

She made a decision that she thought would protect her country.

I can be mad about it or I can respect it. And I think I respect it.

If only Wrath would take the same outlook and forgive me already.

But I guess that begs the question: have I forgiven him?

I look over my shoulder at him and his gaze immediately darts to me. There's an unreadable expression on his face, but it makes me shiver, nonetheless.

"I'm pleased to stand up here today," Naomi goes on, "and inform you all that we have a solution to the scourge that is the Demon King." She pulls back and gestures with a hand at Chaos, and the Demon King's brother steps forward with a sheepish grin.

He's wearing a camel-brown blazer that diminishes the cut of his biceps. There's a navy-blue tie around his neck that goes well with the white and blue plaid shirt beneath.

The round tortoiseshell glasses that sit on the bridge of his nose hide the gleam of his steely gray eyes.

"Good morning, everyone. You're all probably wondering who I am." He ducks his head, lets some heat come to his cheeks as if he's embarrassed or shy to be there. "My name is Charles"—I snort—"and not to alarm any of you, but I'm Wrath's brother."

There's a sharp intake of breath from the assembled press.

Chaos holds up his hand. "I know. I know how that sounds. But hear me out."

It's like he's studied us, like he knows just what to say and how to say it. Wrath could never stand at that podium and look sheepish and say things like *hear me out* in that reluctant tone of voice.

Chaos is a villain of a different sort.

The kind you never see coming.

And I brought him here like the stubborn idiot I am.

That seed of guilt takes root in my chest and unfurls its arms.

My mom likes to say guilt is for suckers and priests and that the only purpose guilt serves is to make us weak or powerful, depending on which end you're on.

"You can't change the past," she's said to me more than once. "No sense dwelling on it."

But there's no doubt that one of the biggest reasons we're here in this situation is because of me.

If only Ciri were still alive so I could ask her what the hell she was thinking.

It felt like she knew what she was doing, that she'd already witnessed the future. I had blind faith in her and Sirene.

But how the hell can this be a good thing? This all feels like a horrible mistake.

"I want to assure you," Chaos says, "that I'm here to help. As

Wrath's brother, I know him very well. Sometimes he throws a tantrum"—the press lets out nervous laughter—"and I'm usually the one there to clean up the mess."

Even though Wrath has already watched this news coverage, I can still sense his vibrating rage. But when I look over at him, his face is blank.

Is it the connection between us? I don't know how I know it, but this news conference is like nettles beneath his skin. It feels like he's on the brink of smashing things.

"I want to help," Chaos tells the crowd. "I *can* help."

Spoken like a true politician.

"I know trusting me will take a considerable amount of proof on my end and I'm willing to put in the hard work so you'll know exactly who I am, and that I'm here to set right what my brother has wronged."

Goosebumps lift on my arms as Wrath's anger sinks a weight in my gut.

"Now, if you have questions," Chaos says, "I'm here to answer."

He calls on someone in the press assembly, a twenty-something woman wearing a pale pink hijab. "As you may know," she says, "Wrath has killed a great many of our soldiers. Can you speak to why he's done so and furthermore, why we should believe you when you say you won't?"

"That's an excellent question." Chaos speaks to the reporter, but I get the clear impression he's speaking directly to Wrath. "My brother can be reckless and stubborn and sometimes he doesn't think through his actions."

The darkness kicks up around us as Wrath's magic writhes in the air.

"And if I'm being honest," Chaos says, "my brother has always been a little bloodthirsty. And I can assure you, I am not."

"No, it's just power he's after," Wrath says behind me.

"I don't wish to harm anyone," Chaos adds.

"I've seen enough." I turn to Wrath. His irritation and anger are almost a living, breathing thing in the room and it's buzzing along my skin like an electrical current. "Shut it off."

"Is it too much for you to face, *dieva*?" Wrath challenges.

"No, I think it's too much for you."

He inhales through his nose, jaw flexing.

"Arthur," I say.

There's a long pause as Arthur hesitates and Wrath faces off with me.

And then Wrath blinks, pulls away, and stalks from the room.

I race after him.

"Tell me how to beat him." I come up alongside him, but my pace is still at a power walk just to keep up with his long strides. "Tell me what to do and I'll do it."

His brow furrows into a scowl. "Now you want to help?"

"I made a mistake." He says nothing. "And so did you."

He comes to an abrupt stop and I have to backpedal to face him.

The darkness pulls in again and I can't tell if it's just his magic or the norrow coming to slam me on the floor again.

I need to figure out how to get these cuffs off my wrists so I at least have a fighting chance of defending myself.

"Nothing has changed," he says. "I still need you to bind yourself to me so that I have the *animus* within my possession. Since you are the *animus*, that means you."

I knew that ultimately it would come to this.

I've had a lot of time to think it over while stuck in that dank hole.

I don't know enough about magic or power or gods or Alius

to know what I might be losing by binding myself to the Demon King.

But I know that I can't outrun him and I can't outrun myself.

Sooner or later I'm going to have to face the fact that I'm not who I thought I was, that everything about my life has changed, and that if I want to move forward, I have to start accepting those things.

"Maybe we can come to an agreement," I say as my heart drums in my chest. My head says this is the right move, but the rest of me wants to vomit.

"I'm listening."

"I have contingencies and questions."

He goes stoic on me again. "Go on."

"In Alius, do women frequent your bed?"

A sliver of surprise comes to his eyes, softening the bite of his scowl. "That's one of your questions?"

"Yes."

"Why does it matter?"

"If I'm to spend the rest of my life bound to you, I want to know the lay of the land."

"By understanding the number of women I invite into my bed?"

"By the number of women you fuck, yes." I want to be real clear on what we're talking about here.

He leans against the stone wall behind him, looking as casual as can be, like we're just two people having a flirty conversation somewhere and not discussing something as profound as a magical marriage.

"Before my betrothal," he says, "the number was many. Afterward, fewer."

"And lately?"

"Lately," he says, "just one."

I scream at every muscle and fiber in my body not to react to the triumph of that statement. Like what I want to be doing is running down the hallway hooting at the ceiling.

But I'm a mature, respectable woman.

But also FUCK YES. The Demon King is mine. Even if he does irritate the hell out of me.

There is no sense fighting it anymore. I've been tethered to him not by choice, but by circumstance, so I might as well make the most of it. And if I'm to make the most of it, I'll stake my claim, goddammit.

"And what about after?" I keep my voice level. "After all of this?"

"I haven't thought that far in advance."

I cross my arms. "Then think about it now."

"Are you asking me to stay faithful to you and only you?"

"Well...would you be okay with other men in my bed?"

Nostrils flaring, he lurches upright, shoulders rocking back. "There will be no other men in your bed."

Don't react. Don't react.

Now I'm parkouring off the walls in my mind palace.

Stay cool.

"Why not?" I ask.

"Because you are mine."

"I'm not your possession."

"I've called *dieva*," he says, a little smug. "In Alius, if anyone dared to touch you, it would be within my right to cut off their hands and shove them down their throat."

"Is that the only reason? Because of some barbaric claiming practice?"

He glances away. His black t-shirt sinks on his shoulders, exposing a whirl of his black demon mark as it winds over his collarbone.

I tighten my arms over my chest trying to keep myself from

running my fingers over it just to watch him shiver beneath my touch.

"No man will come to your bed," he says when he turns back. "That answer is final."

"So what, you can sleep with whoever you want, but I can't?"

"Is this one of your contingencies?" he asks.

"Yes," I answer because why the hell not.

"Is there more?"

"I want to stay here, in my world."

"No."

While this answer is not really surprising, I'd hoped otherwise.

I don't know the first thing about living in another world.

It feels too much like starting at a new high school where you don't understand the cliques or the rules and you just have to figure it out as you go.

But after living half my life with my mom, bouncing all over the world, that's a situation I know how to navigate extremely well. Maybe I can manage a new world without too much trouble.

"Can I go back and forth?" I ask.

He considers this for a second and then, "That would require permanently opening the gateway. Is that what you want?"

Fuck. If we were playing chess, he's just cornered me.

"No, I suppose not. But can you at least figure out a way for me to visit from time to time?"

"I can."

"But will you?"

He narrows his eyes again. "For you, *dieva*, yes, I will. Are we finished?"

"The people I love and care about."

"What about them?"

"You will not lay a finger on them. In no way will they be harmed. Ever."

He doesn't need time to consider this contingency, but his words are cold, nonetheless. "Your precious mortals will remain unscathed."

"And the women in your bed?"

As if I'd forget.

He pushes away from the wall and stalks toward me. I take a step back.

"I want an heir someday," he says. "Are you willing to bear my child?"

"Umm..."

Even though he insinuated that he'd pump someone full of his demon seed someday—that impregnating a woman with demon royalty was brutal fucking—it never once crossed my mind that he'd want that woman to be me.

Sure, I'd like to test the brutal fucking part, because I'm always up for a wild ride, but...children? I never gave them much thought. And after doing family photography for so long, I started to think I didn't want them.

But with the Demon King?

The thought makes me glow a little inside.

Before he showed up, I'd been empty. Looking back, I see it for what it was: I thought I just needed to find a path, do some internal growing, but being with Wrath...I've never felt so *awake*.

"All right, yes," I answer. "I'll bear you an heir." My voice catches on 'heir' and he hears it.

"Are you sure that's what you want?"

Now he's giving me an out?

And if I said no?

But I won't. I don't want to.

"Yes. I'm sure."

"Then my answer is this—if you bind yourself to me, bear my heir, then I will only bury my cock in your tight little pussy. Does that suffice?"

Heat flares in my face and then travels down my belly and to my clit. I get a flash of what we did last night, the feel of his hands on my hips and his cock shoved inside of me.

I know he can smell me now and can probably sense where my lusty thoughts have gone.

"Okay," I breathe out.

"Okay?" He lifts a brow.

"I'll bind myself to you."

My heart drums hard in my chest as the panic sets in. Have I made the right decision? Will I regret this for the rest of my life? Do I even understand what I'm doing?

Am I seriously considering going to another world with the Demon King?

I'm tired of running and I'm tired of fighting him and if I'm totally honest, I'm tired of pretending that I hate the thought of being only his.

"No more games, *dieva*," he warns.

"No more games."

He licks his bottom lip, then drags it in with a rake of his teeth as he considers me. I get the distinct impression he's waiting for another shoe to drop.

I hold out my hand. "Let's shake on it."

He regards me with the hint of an amused smile on his ravaging mouth, then slips his hand into mine and shakes.

It's done.

I've agreed to marry the Demon King.

"So how do we do this?"

"We need a witch," he tells me as he backtracks to the Bourbon Room.

"Kat?" I ask, chasing after him.

"Arthur," he calls as he reenters the room. "Rain and I are going to House Roman. You make sure things are in order. Lauren."

She launches herself from the couch. I wouldn't be surprised if she saluted him. "Yes?"

"Take off your shirt."

Lauren regards him with a warring look on her face. She wants to obey, but she clearly knows where this is going.

"Lauren." His voice rumbles and the darkness kicks up, tendrils undulating in the air.

She yanks the plain black tee over her head and tosses it to me. I catch it in a ball.

Wrath turns to me, grabs the hem of my Demon Slut shirt, and unceremoniously relieves me of it. He stalks over to Lauren and hands it to her. "Put it on."

She glowers at him but slips it on anyway.

"When we return," he tells her, "she will be a queen and you will treat her like one." She takes a step back and Wrath follows, running her into the wall. A yelp escapes her throat. "No more games, Lauren."

"Yes, my king."

"Louder."

"Yes, my king!"

He swivels around, satisfied, and comes for me next.

I think he's tripled in size because I swear to god we all shrink around him when he demands we fall in line. "And you," he says to me, "you will act like a queen."

"Okay."

He stops a few inches from me and regards me with cool expectation.

I huff out a breath. "Yes, my king."

"Good girl," he says and for some reason, the praise hits me square in the chest.

Lauren didn't get a good girl. Ha.

He slips his arm around my waist and pulls me into him as his dark magic kicks up in a writhing mist.

"Ready, *dieva*?"

"Yes," I say with as much confidence as I can muster.

CHAPTER
FIVE

Wrath deposits us in a garden with a massive estate house in front of us and a harbor behind us. I immediately recognize the harbor as Chantilly Harbor in Saint Sabine.

Gus and I come to the city often and I love Second Quarter the most. It reminds me of a quainter New Orleans.

Somewhere beyond the house, jazz music plays from a street corner and laughter and revelry rises above it, despite the early hour of the day.

Much like in Norton Harbor, there's a paved boardwalk that runs along Chantilly, but there's far more greenery here shielding the garden from the prying eyes of pedestrians and tourists.

I gaze up at the estate house.

Gus and I have gone on the boardwalk many times before and I've always admired this house from afar having no idea it belonged to a vampire. Now that I know it, I can't unsee it. It *looks* like a vampire's house.

Wrath takes my hand and guides me through the garden over cobblestone paths mottled with moss. There are hundreds of flower varieties blooming in the garden in shades of pink and purple and orange and yellow. What a dream.

"This place is stunning," I say as Wrath takes us to French doors.

"If you think this is amazing, you should see the royal garden in Alius. It puts this one to shame."

Now he's piqued my interest. "You never talk about Alius."

"I just did."

"Before, I guess. To me."

He looks down at me. "I never saw a reason to...before."

Before I agreed to marry him.

I blink rapidly and break eye contact, suddenly flustered.

I don't know why. I don't know why him sharing details about his home is somehow more profound than him sticking his cock inside of me.

But it is.

And now I'm hungry for more.

Hand on the door handle, he turns it and pushes in, not waiting for an invitation.

We enter into a cool, hushed darkness.

It's eerily quiet.

"Where is everyone?"

"Vampires sleep during the day," Wrath reminds me.

"Right. Of course."

"Kat," Wrath yells.

"Shhhh! If they're all sleeping—"

"I'm here." Kat appears in an arched doorway, looking smashing as usual. She's wearing a pantsuit today in a deep shade of emerald. The shoulders are sculpted like thorns, the collar plunging, showing off her cleavage.

Her dark hair is done in soft waves, her long bangs framing her face.

As seems to be her signature, her plump lips are a bright shade of red.

"She's agreed," Wrath says and lets me go.

"Has she?" Kat arches a brow at me, regarding me from beneath the fan of her lashes.

"She has," I say.

"Mmmm." Kat curls her hands around her hips. "I will never understand you two. At each other's throats one minute, marrying each other the next."

"It's not marriage," Wrath argues. "It's a binding. Much different."

"Is it?" Kat turns that sharp brow his way.

"Yes," he says on a growl.

I don't see much of a difference. In some ways, this is bigger than a marriage because I can't divorce his ass if I grow tired of his nagging.

"So how do we bind ourselves?" I ask. "Is there a ceremony? Do we need witnesses? Should we wait for the others to wake? And most importantly, will there be cake?"

"It's not a spectacle," Wrath argues. "We do it now. The sooner the better. And no cake."

I pout at him. He scowls.

"Come this way." Kat swivels on her heels.

We follow her out into an arched hallway where soft inset lighting guides us through the shuttered house.

We pass several pieces of art in gilded frames. I know from growing up with an artist that several of these paintings are presumed missing and are worth millions.

I think I heard someone say Rhys Roman is a billionaire. And apparently a serious art collector.

Kat turns into another hall and a large-scale photograph of Háifoss waterfall catches my eye. The image is portrait format with the falls taking center stage surrounded by green moss and craggy outcroppings. Mist hangs heavy in the air, turning much of the photograph hazy, almost like a painting.

"That's one of my mother's photographs from Iceland."

Kat stops to glance at the image contained in an ornate black frame. "Is it? I didn't realize."

I get a little flare of pride seeing my mom's work in the hall of a billionaire's house. A vampire no less. Wait till I tell her. She's going to flip.

Kat keeps walking and Wrath sets his hand at the small of my back, spurring me on.

We finally turn into a smaller room, darkened with black shutters that are turned down so slatted rays of light pour in over the room.

It smells like Kat in here, like expensive perfume mixed with exotic herbs and a fair dash of earned pride. There's a long worktable across from the door and an entire wall of cabinets to the right with glass-fronted doors. The collection of jars inside stokes my curiosity and I immediately go to it, scanning the contents. Except, all of the labels are handwritten in a language I don't understand.

"Do witches really use herbs and toads and eyes of newt to do their magic?"

Wrath picks up a corked jar. He scrutinizes whatever is inside.

"I use magic without all the accoutrements," Kat answers, "but some things can help focus, bind, or amplify certain magics. Most witches don't need all of this, but we like it none-theless."

"Do you need it for a binding?"

"We'll use it," she says as she comes up beside me. "Just to be sure. Are you sure?" She lifts a brow, scrutinizes my reaction.

"Yes. I don't entirely understand what it means to be the *animus*, and I don't know how to use it so it seems silly to keep it to myself while Chaos causes...well, chaos. And anyway, the *animus* doesn't belong to me. The power belongs to the Demon King."

Kat frowns. "So by that logic you belong to him?"

I sense him watching me.

"Are you trying to talk me out of it?"

"I'm trying to understand."

"You're bound to Rhys Roman, aren't you?"

She crosses her arms over her chest, sharp red fingernails curling around her biceps. "I am."

"Do you regret it?"

"Not a chance. He's my best friend, as much as he can be an asshole."

"I know that plight well."

I practically hear Wrath roll his eyes.

"Rhys and House Roman are my family. But"—she cants her head, waves of her hair cascading over her shoulders—"I'm bound to House Roman by oath and blood. This"—she points a sharp nail at Wrath—"this is different."

"How?"

"I could, theoretically, get myself out of my position. My oath is much like those cuffs on your wrists. They can break. What you're doing, binding yourself to the Demon King in this way? That's like putting an orange in a blender and pressing the button. That orange is not coming out the same way ever again."

Goosebumps lift on my arms.

I never would have thought an analogy about fruit could sound so profoundly eerie and sinister.

"What's different about your binding from mine?"

The look she gives me is almost sympathetic. "Everything."

∾

First, Kat takes off the magical cuffs, then undoes the binding she put on me since the spell won't work with all of it still in place. Undoing the binding is nothing more than a few whispered words and the snap of her fingers and suddenly the power rushes back in like a dam that's been broken.

My eyes slip closed and I breathe out with a sigh.

It's like a hot shower after too many nights in the cold.

I'm no longer numb.

"Better?" she asks when I pry my eyes open again.

"Much."

I rub my sore wrists, the skin chafed and red. God, it feels good to have those things off.

I guess we've taken another step in the direction of holy matrimony, because Wrath trusts me enough not to have my magic bound.

I still plan to zap his ass someday soon. He fucking deserves it.

It takes Kat about fifteen minutes to prepare for the binding and my palms start sweating three minutes into her work.

I pace the room.

Wrath leans against the worktable watching me, completely unfazed.

I'm trying not to look at him, but it's impossible not to feel his presence when he's in a room.

He says nothing and lets me freak out.

What am I doing?

I like being an orange.

But orange juice is really great too.

Fuck, now I'm thinking in riddles.

"*Dieva,*" he says.

I stop pacing to catch his gaze. He's unreadable, face blank. Does he feel it too? This trembling on the horizon?

"We can't go back to being oranges after this," I tell him.

"I know."

"Do you?" I swivel on my heel and start pacing again. "Maybe this entire time I've been freaking out about being bound to you and you haven't properly considered what it'll mean to be bound to me. I mean...will I age? You certainly don't. What if I become a saggy old bag someday and you're stuck with me, your rotten, sour orange juice?"

There's a snap of air, a kiss of a breeze on the back of my neck.

When I turn, he's there, just an inch from me, filling my space. "I'm not worried."

It's a simple statement, and ludicrous, if I'm honest—*he should be worried*—but it settles my nerves just the same.

"Just to clarify...which part are you not worried about? Being bound to me? Me turning into a saggy old bag?"

The corner of his mouth lifts. There is something profoundly enjoyable about getting the Demon King to laugh. "Both," he answers. "All of your worries. Set them aside. There is only one way for us to go and that's forward."

"That's deep. You should put that on Demon King merch."

He laughs again. I warm.

"I'm ready when you are," Kat says.

My heart drums in my chest. "All right. I guess I'm ready too."

Wrath nods, acknowledging me and my consent.

Kat takes two giant abalone shells over to the worktable. The inside of the shells shines pearlescent beneath a mixture of herbs. "I need a lock of hair from both of you."

"Here, let me," I say and reach over and pluck several jet-black hairs from Wrath's skull.

He curses, growls, then winds several strands of my hair around his index finger and yanks them out by the root.

"Ouch!" I rub at the sore spot. "I think you were rougher than I was."

"I will always be rougher, *dieva*."

Kat gives us an exasperated look and then takes the hair and sets it in the herbs in each shell. Next, she flattens her hands over them and whispers something foreign.

There's a soft WHUMP and green fire ignites beneath her hands, flames licking around her knuckles. She doesn't flinch and the only scent on the air is that of burning herbs.

When she pulls her hand away, there is a small stone in each shell. One is opaque white, the other shining black like obsidian.

"That's interesting," she says as she takes the stones into each hand.

"Which part?"

She brings the opaque stone into a stream of light. "They're different colors. It's just unexpected."

"Were they supposed to be the same?" Wrath asks.

"I would assume they would be. You and Rain, your power, it's all from the same current, you know? I would expect them to be the same."

I cross my arms over my chest. "Is it bad that they aren't?"

"You want the truth or a guess?"

"The truth," Wrath says.

"I don't know."

"And the guess?" I ask.

Kat looks at the stone again. "I don't know."

"Okay. Awesome."

"We'll move forward regardless," Wrath says.

"Of course." Kat clears a spot on the worktable and sets aside the shells. "This is one of those spells that requires us to be quick. Like cutting a baby from a womb. We need to move once the blood runs."

"Will there be blood?"

"Something of this magnitude? Yes. Absolutely." She grabs a length of black charcoal and starts scribbling fiercely on the worktop. When she's finished, there are two identical circles with rune symbols inside. "This is how this will work." She picks up my opaque stone. "We cut open both of your palms. Stone goes in one hand. The other hand will touch the grounding symbols here." She taps at the charcoal. "Once you've connected with the grounding symbols, you'll bring the stones to one another, right over your hearts. The spell will be kindled at that point. You'll feel the current open between you and you will be bound. Any questions?"

"Do I say anything? 'I do,' maybe?"

Kat laughs. "Nope. The power is in the blood. Not the words."

"Got it."

I never gave my wedding day much thought. I've always liked being alone and I've never been in a relationship that gave me marriage vibes.

But if I had been one of those girls that daydreamed about her special day, this wouldn't have been it. Not even close.

"Take your shirts off," Kat instructs.

I pull my t-shirt off and toss it aside.

Wrath grabs his at the back of the neck and slips it over his head in one swift motion, muscles flexing along his shoulders, abs contracting with the movements. He tosses the shirt and stands half naked in the slatted daylight.

I feel Kat appreciating the view beside me and without thinking, I scowl over at her, damn near bristling.

"Calm down," she says. "As if I would be brave enough to cross you."

That pulls me upright and the territorial bitch immediately relaxes.

Brave enough to cross me? Kat is a vicious, gorgeous, badass witch.

I'm just a photographer from a tourist town.

But I detect no bullshit on her face. She's fucking serious.

Grabbing a blade from inside an ornate box, Kate takes my hand in hers. "Both palms. Got it?"

"Yup."

She slices my first hand and I bite against a hiss. The pain is immediate and sharp but fades quickly as blood wells in the wound. She moves quickly to my other hand, cutting a near identical wound.

When she turns to Wrath, he's already got his hands up, blood dripping down his wrists.

"Right. Connected on a physical level. I forgot," Kat says. "Then let's finish the job and make it official on all levels. Ready?"

Wrath looks at me. There's no question on his face, but there's a flash of doubt in his eyes as if he's waiting for me to back out, run away.

I'm not running this time.

I've made my choice.

"All right," Kat says. "Then let's begin."

CHAPTER
SIX

IN UNISON, WRATH AND I BRING OUR BLEEDING HANDS TO THE grounding symbols Kat sketched on the worktable. Mine is my right hand and his is his left.

The second our blood hits the charcoal, the symbols burn bright green just like Kat's magic.

There's a heaviness that crawls up my arm and a tugging pressure beneath the palm of my hand that feels very much like an anchor.

My white stone is clutched in my left hand, now wet with my blood. Wrath has his captured between his thumb and forefinger as we wait.

Kat closes her eyes and whispers a string of words I can't comprehend. I smell the sweetness that I now attribute to her magic and it reminds me of an herb garden my mom had for a summer, like basil and bergamot.

"Now. Now!" Kat says, snapping her fingers at us.

Wrath and I reach across the short distance between us and press our stones to each other's heart.

I feel the coolness of the bloody stone first, then the heat of his touch.

And a second later, a gale force shoots across the room. Loose paper flutters in the wind and the slats of the shutters flap loudly as my hair is tossed in my face.

"Is this normal?" I shout.

"Don't let go!" Kat yells.

There's a liquid rushing down my arm as Wrath's stone burns at my chest, as heat and energy charge toward me. Wrath grits his teeth together as the monster comes to his face, sharp and sharper still. His fingers claw at my skin as if he's holding on to me for dear life.

I can't catch my breath. It's like I've turned my face into a tornado, all the oxygen sucked from my lungs.

The heat spreads through the rest of my body, nerves and muscle crackling. My skin grows taut like I've been out in the sun too long, like it could split open at the slightest touch.

Green light flares beneath my palm as the grounding symbol reenergizes, as if it can feel my grip on it slipping.

Wrath adjusts his stance, planting his boots to the floor and the wood beneath him buckles.

I flinch. The wind kicks up, knocking a stack of books off the table. They thud to the floor, pages flapping.

Kat hurries to the wall of cabinets and starts opening doors, rummaging inside.

"What's happening?" I yell.

"Don't let go," Wrath says.

"I won't."

The veins in Wrath's hand stand out, swelling beneath his skin as his knuckles turn white.

The connection between us vibrates and the air balloons around us with a milky green haze.

The door bangs open. Rhys Roman appears in the glow of light with Dane and Emery behind him.

"What the fuck is happening?" Rhys asks.

NIKKI ST. CROWE

"Don't come into the room!" Kat yells.

"Should we be worried?" Dane shouts back.

Kat keeps rummaging.

"Wrath?"

His eyes are locked on me. "Don't let go, *dieva*," he says again, but his voice is missing its usual grit and it doesn't feel like a warning to me so much as a plea. As if I'm the only thing keeping him from being swept away.

"I won't," I tell him again. "I'm not leaving your side."

The wind picks up. Rhys puts his arm over his face, shielding his eyes as a bottle of herbs knocks over and smashes on the ground, sending dozens of dried sprigs flying through the air.

"Kat!" he yells again.

"I found it!" She hurries over to us, a metal rod in hand.

"What is that?" I ask just as she positions it over my forehead and everything goes black.

I WAKE with a start and it takes me a second to come back to awareness, to feel Wrath's body beneath mine, his arms wrapped around me.

There's a pulsing energy running between us like a heat wave over hot asphalt.

That's different.

I look around and realize we're back in the main room in House Roman. Kate, Rhys, Dane, and Emery are in front of me, watching me.

Wrath is sitting in an overstuffed chair, me nestled in his lap and the feel of him this close, his touch gentle, is enough to send butterflies migrating through my stomach.

"What happened?" I sit forward and Wrath spreads his legs,

58

letting me sit between his thighs. His hands are still on me almost like he's afraid to let me go.

Kat comes forward. "Do you feel all right?" She bows at the waist to scrutinize my face while her hands hover in the air around me.

"Headachy," I admit. "What happened?" I ask again.

"Well..." She frowns at me, then straightens, hands curling around the hourglass shape of her hips. "You were more powerful than I anticipated."

I press at the spot between my brows. "Huh?"

"When I drew the grounding symbols, I put more weight on Wrath's side. He's more powerful than you. Or he should be. But apparently he isn't."

I'm immediately reminded of Ciri's last words right before Wrath killed her.

You're no longer the most powerful person in the room, she said to him.

Meaning me. Meaning *I* was the most powerful one.

I thought it was just bullshit. One last dig before she lost her life.

But now, with this...was she serious?

"I had the balance wrong," Kat admits. "I apologize for that."

I glance at him over my shoulder. His eyes are narrowed as he meets my gaze. There is nothing overtly menacing about him but I can feel something foreign thrumming around me.

It takes me a second to realize it's Wrath's unease.

It's almost a living, breathing thing. Like I could reach out and run my fingers through it, watch the air bristle and part.

I'm more powerful than he is and he's uneasy about it.

The sands are shifting beneath us.

Suddenly, I don't feel so steady.

This was supposed to be a good thing. It wasn't supposed to reveal more weak spots in our relationship.

"So did it work? The binding?" I ask.

"You tell me." He tips his chin at me. "What do you feel?"

"I do feel different," I admit. "Beyond the headache, that is. Almost like—"

Anticipation.

Eagerness.

I can feel him so acutely it's like he's living in my heart and in my head.

I lurch off the chair, goosebumps rising along my skin.

He stands beside me, clearly on edge.

"Do you feel it?" I ask him quietly.

He grits his teeth, sucks in a breath, then, "Yes."

"What do you feel from me?"

"Fear. Worry."

"Fuck," I say beneath my breath. "You didn't tell me we'd have no secrets."

"I didn't know. I've never done this before, *dieva*."

I pace away from him and he comes after me, aching with the need to be near me and then there's a quick flash of—

I whirl around to face him. He reels back like I smacked him.

Was that...

No. *No.*

It wasn't love. The Demon King has no heart.

But there is an ache in my chest right now that feels like it, but I don't know if it's him or me or maybe both.

Fuck. Binding ourselves together was just supposed to be a minor detail, a slip of paper and nothing more.

We're not supposed to actually care for each other. Right?

Tears burn in my eyes and I rub my hands up and down my arms.

This is too much too fast.

Shit. I'm freaking out.

"Rhys," Wrath says with a clipped tone of voice.

"Yes?" Rhys comes forward.

"Will Rain be safe in your house if I was to leave?"

"Of course. The house is deeded to a human and Kat has the perimeter spelled."

"Good. Keep her here."

"Wait." I hurry forward but before I can reach him, he's gone.

CHAPTER
SEVEN

I START FOR THE DOOR, THE ONE THAT OPENS ON THE BACK GARDEN where Wrath and I first came in to House Roman.

But before I can turn the handle, Rhys is in front of me.

I'm used to Wrath popping in and out on a whim, but vampire speed is something that still takes me by surprise.

A little yelp bursts from my throat and I stumble back.

"Apologies, Ms. Low, but I can't let you leave." Rhys Roman is no Wrath, but he's still really fucking scary. There's something in the way he moves—not quite ghost-like, but close. Like he moves so fast my eyesight can't keep up, and so his movements are nothing but a blur of color.

"I'm not going to be a prisoner in your house," I say. "I'm done being held captive."

"Not captive," Rhys says and tilts his chiseled jaw at me, a lock of his blond hair falling forward. "Protected. There is a difference."

When he speaks to me, low and evenly with that perfect British accent, I almost want to give in. Almost.

I cross my arms over my chest as the *animus* flares to life. God, does it feel good to have her back.

It's like I can stretch my legs again after being crammed into a closet.

Rhys grits his teeth and throws back his shoulders.

I catch my reflection in the glass in the door—my eyes are glowing embers.

Could a vampire stop me from leaving?

"Rain." Emery comes up beside Rhys and puts her much smaller body in front of the massive vampire. "Why don't you take a walk with me?"

The *animus* immediately retreats and Rhys eases the tension from his shoulders.

"Where?" I ask Emery.

"There's something you might find interesting that Kat and I have been dying to show you."

"What is it?"

"You're overselling it," Kat tells Emery. "It's just books," she says to me.

"Yes, but books are the gateway to knowledge. And you know what Horace Mann said about knowledge? 'Every addition to true knowledge is an addition to human power.'"

Kat screws up her red lips. "Horace Mann was a goddamn prude."

"Wait." Emery blinks. "You knew Horace Mann?"

"Who is Horace Mann?" I ask.

"Can we please stop talking about Horace Mann?" Dane pipes in. "I much prefer we talk about me instead. Do you know what *I* said about knowledge?"

"Oh god." Kat rolls her eyes.

"Nothing. I said nothing about knowledge because I'm not a fucking pretentious twat."

Emery smiles at me and hooks her arm through mine. "Ignore him. He's obnoxious."

"I think what you meant to say, poppet, is, 'He's devastatingly handsome and charming.'"

I snort as Emery drags me away. "How has he not been staked before?"

"Oh, he has. Many times. He's just really good at hiding his heart."

"It's because he doesn't have one." Kat falls into step beside us. "If you tore open his rib cage, you'd find just a stone of hubris."

"Do not leave the house," Rhys calls after us.

"Yes, dear," Emery says over her shoulder.

"I mean it." His voice rumbles behind us.

"Just to be clear—" I start.

"He really does mean it," Emery finishes. "I love the man, but you do not want to cross him. Come. I have a feeling you're going to love the library."

EMERY IS RIGHT.

"Holy shit," I say as I step inside after Emery and Kat push open the thick double doors.

"I feel like Belle in the Beast's library." I gaze around in wonder, craning my neck as I take it all in.

There are two stories with the second floor open to the main floor by a wrought iron railing. A wide set of stairs directly across from the entrance takes you up to a landing where a giant circular window dominates the wall. From there, the stairs branch off left and right to the second story.

On the main floor, several tables fill the space, each with a matching library lamp on top. Vintage sconces cast a soft golden glow around the room, with three massive iron chandeliers above doing the rest of the work to light the space now that the sun has set.

"Kat," Emery says, "will you grab that book on the gods? And I'll go find the one with the—"

"Already on it." Kat starts across the room, her hips swaying, her stilettos silent on the plush Persian rugs.

"Make yourself comfortable," Emery says as she leaves me for the second floor.

I go to the nearest bookcase and run my fingers over the spines. Most of the books seem ancient, bound in leather, the titles stamped in gold and silver. Each shelf has a bronze placard tacked into the wood with a slip of cardstock inside with a printed label. There's 18th century romance and 19th century horror. And then I spot a copy of *Frankenstein* and pull it out, flipping to the front pages.

There's an inscription inside.

DEAREST RHYS,
   Meeting you was a pleasure. A bloody pleasure, indeed.
   Mary Shelley

"THIS IS SIGNED BY MARY SHELLEY!" I yell and the girls laugh.

"If you like that sort of thing," Kat says over her shoulder, "there are signed copies of *Pride & Prejudice*, *Dracula*, *Jane Eyre*, *The Great Gatsby*, *Wuthering Heights*—"

"And Shakespeare, if you can believe it," Emery adds from the second floor.

"They're just sitting here on the shelves? Like...just shoved in with the rest of the normal books?"

"When you're a vampire," Emery says, "they're all normal books."

I return Frankenstein to the shelf, but before I can locate the other signed editions, Kat and Emery return with the books they were searching for.

Kat's book is thin and near pocket-sized. Emery's book is much bigger by comparison. She needs both hands to carry it and when she sets it on the table, it thuds loudly. The title has no inlaid coloring. I run my fingers over it, feeling the hard edges of the stamped letters.

Mythology of Alius.

"What's yours called?" I ask Kat.

She slides hers across the table to me.

The Tale of the Original Gods.

"They're both from Alius," Emery says.

"We think," Kat adds.

Emery opens the cover of her book and the spine creaks. "After the Demon King arrived, we all got curious about his origins."

"Mostly it was Emery who got curious."

"I like my history." She flips through the pages, careful with the thin paper. "They've always known about Alius." She tips her head at Kat.

"You did?"

Kat shrugs and pulls out one of the chairs. "We thought it was an urban legend. A fairytale."

"So I knew there had to be something about it in the library," Emery goes on. She turns several more pages and I catch sight of black and white illustrations, some depicting battles, others of gorgeous creatures surrounded by more beauty. "I started doing research, trying to see what I could learn about Alius and the Demon King should we need to—"

"Murder him," Kat cuts in.

Emery sends her a sharp look. "No. Defend ourselves against him."

"AKA murder him."

"But you're allied with him," I point out. "You literally did his bidding and bound me."

Kat lifts another shoulder in this casual, flippant way she has that should be irritating but isn't. "I do as Rhys wishes and Rhys wishes to cooperate with Wrath. I clearly had my own opinions about it. If it was up to me, I would not have bound you. I like you. I like you more than I like Wrath. But the truth of the matter is, I hold no loyalty to you. I don't really know you. I've known Rhys for centuries."

"Wait...you're immortal too?"

She smiles at me with a cheeky flare of pride in her eyes. "Comes with being a Redheart witch. We have dominion over magic of the flesh. Means I get to keep this gorgeous body forever so long as I don't lose my head."

"Is that what kind of witch Sirene is?"

"I couldn't tell you," Kat admits. "But the scars on her face make me doubt she's a Redheart. If she was, she would have healed herself."

"She told me she got those scars from Wrath."

"Oh?" Kat lifts her brows in surprise as she thinks that over. "Actually...that makes sense." She picks up her book and flips through several pages, then taps her finger on the printed text. "'...no man, woman, child, or animal is invincible against the power of the original gods. He who angers the gods will forever bear the mark of their insolence.'"

I frown. "The original gods...so, the triad?"

"That's just scratching the surface." Emery spins her book around to face me. "Read this."

"'In the beginning, there was only Night and Day—the Dark God and the Bright Goddess. One did not exist without the other, and yet they did not exist together, passing each other only briefly at the horizon.'

"'It was at that passing that the Dark God learned of the Goddess's warmth and light and he hungered for it more and more every day until finally the God created the Moon.'

"'The Goddess filled his night with light, but she would fade from him, and worse, she was *cold*.'

"'The God's hunger persisted. His desire for Day consumed him until he was so ravenous for her, he devoured her in the sky, stealing all of her light.'

"'It was through their consummation that the world was born.'"

I look up. Emery and Kat are staring at me. "That's some heavy mythology."

Emery reaches over and flips a few more pages. "Read this."

There's a symbol at the top of the page that looks like an eclipse, which makes sense with the story. Night consumed Day.

I keep reading. "'As the world grew, Night watched Day give birth to more and more. To the grass in the fields and the flowers in the meadows, the birds in the sky, the trees in the forests. At night, her moon controlled the ocean, swayed the seas. The Dark God grew jealous of her power and her dominion over all that lived and breathed. He wanted that power for himself. He was the King and he would be the only ruler of the world.'"

Dread runs along my spine, raising the hair at the back of my neck.

"'Night tricked Day. He lured her from the sky and trapped her beneath the earth. She raged and raged until she bore a mountain and her rage spewed into the sky, shrouding the world in darkness.'"

I push the book away. "I can admire the symbolism," I say. "The sun and the moon, the eclipses, the volcano. But how does this relate to Wrath?"

"The stones," Kat says. "The stones that contain the Demon King's power, right? The triad? They're said to be from the Dark Father God, but I think the story is wrong. They belong to the Goddess. It was the God who stole them."

I frown at her, trying to digest what she's saying. "It's still only a story."

"But is it?" Emery sits in the chair beside me, but she's sideways so she faces me. "Think about it. The stones are black, like volcanic rock."

I only saw one briefly when Chaos stole the *oculus* from Wrath, but even before then, Wrath described them to me as being black, carved with the old language.

My chest tightens as this weird feeling invades my body, a feeling like there might be weight to what they're saying.

"The Demon King rules with borrowed power," Kat says.

I snort. "That's not true."

Emery and Kat share a look.

"What? What is it?"

Emery rakes her teeth over her bottom lip.

Kat says, "Night and Day have many names in the mythology just like the gods and goddesses that belong to your Greek and Roman mythology."

"Okay?"

Emery grabs Kat's tiny book and flips to the back to a glossary, then hands it to me.

I skim the section.

DAY | Bright Goddess
   Known also as Sun, Sun Goddess, Divine Mother, Giver of Life, Sola, Borna, Mater Dea, Reginae, Reignyabit, Reign

. . .

MY HEART STOPS. A cold sweat breaks out along my hairline.

I immediately jump to the memory of Wrath at my mom's cottage, the way he reacted to my name, how he insinuated it was supposed to be Reign and not Rain.

I just thought he was pissed about Sirene helping to name me something that literally meant stealing his throne from him.

But now—

I look up. "This doesn't mean anything. I don't...I *mean*...I'm just some rando girl."

They're both staring at me with pinched eyes, furrowed brows.

"Right?"

When they don't answer, I slam the book shut. "I'm not some reincarnated goddess or whatever. Is that what you're saying? I'm just a photographer from a tourist town with a new age mother who likes tea and patchouli and...and I drink too much. I mean, does a goddess really drink too much wine and fall asleep on her balcony so she burns in the sun? No." I lurch away from the table. "This is just a story."

Kat stands up. She doesn't approach me. I think she knows I'm on the verge of running. "If it was just a story," she says, "then why are you more powerful than the Demon King?"

"You messed up the spell."

She snorts. "I take offense to that. I don't mess up."

"Then it was because he lost the *oculus*."

"You have one stone. He has one stone. It should be equal at the very least."

"It's because I weakened him."

Emery finally cuts in. "Listen, we're not going to jump to any conclusions, okay?"

"Okay." Tears are suddenly burning in my eyes. "Have you told Wrath any of this?"

"No," Emery answers.

"Please don't."

"He must know that—" Kat starts, and Emery cuts her off with a sharp look.

"We're not going to mention it to Wrath," Emery says. "We just thought it might be fun to know more about the legends and Alius."

Distantly, I'm aware that Emery is just telling me what I want to hear, but I can't handle this. Not right now. Now when I just bound myself to the Demon King and I felt the connection between us thrum with...

And then he abandoned me here.

That's because he knows, the voice in the back of my head says. *He has to know the mythology behind his power.*

And now Kat's spell proves it.

Fuck me.

CHAPTER
EIGHT

WE'RE EVENTUALLY PULLED AWAY FROM THE BOOKS BY THE SOUND OF A child yelling.

"That sounds like Gabe," Emery says.

"Who's Gabe?" I follow the women from the library and back to the main living space. There's a little boy spinning round and round on one of the barstools while a woman behind the bar empties the trash.

"Gabriel Luis Visser," the woman says. "Get off that stool this instant."

"I'm breaking a record, Ma!" he yells.

"Gabe." Kat comes up beside him and flicks her wrist and the stool lurches to a stop. Gabe sways as if he's still spinning and has lost his equilibrium.

"Ahhh come on, witchy woman!"

"Gabriel!" the woman says again.

"It's all right, Lisa," Kat says. "You know we tolerate this little demon because we love you the most."

Gabe snorts and hops down. "Ma ain't your favorite. I am. You tolerate Ma because you love me."

Lisa comes around the bar with a bag of trash clutched in

her hand. "I swear to god, young man, you will be the death of me."

Gabe laughs and darts away as his mom reaches out for him.

Except he slams right into Wrath.

Gabe bounces back and Wrath's hand snaps out, taking a fistful of Gabe's shirt, catching him before he falls. It doesn't take the Demon King any effort at all. He barely moves a muscle.

Eyes wide, Gabe looks up. "Holy shit," he says. "The Demon King."

Lisa makes the sign of the cross over her body.

No one moves.

Gabe just hangs there, dangling by his shirt.

Do I step in? Do I try to get the Demon King away from the poor innocent little boy?

Wrath said he wanted his own children, but that tells me little about how he actually is around them.

Using Gabe's shirt, Wrath pulls the boy closer so they're face to face. Gabe holds his breath.

"Respect your mother," Wrath says in his deep, menacing voice.

Gabe exhales in a rush. "Okay. Sure. Whatever you say Mr. King. I mean, sir."

"He's really harmless," Kat says. "Just a bit of a pain in the ass from time to time."

Wrath lets Gabe go and the kid stumbles back before finding his footing and straightening his shirt. "I'm not a pain in the ass."

"Yes, you are." We all turn to Rhys at the sound of his voice as he comes into the room and goes behind the bar. He grabs something from beneath the counter. It isn't until he's drinking it back, lips stained red, that I realize it's a bottle of blood.

Ugh.

I'm glad Wrath doesn't have to do that.

No, he just bathes in the blood of his enemies.

"Hey Mr. Demon King," Gabe says, his bravado back. "You think I can see those shadow soldiers? They're so cool, man. I wish I had those guys around. I'd be kicking asses left and right." He curls his hands into fists and punches at imagined enemies.

"Gabriel!" Lisa shrieks.

"Sorry, Ma," he says looking sheepish this time. But even that isn't enough to deter him. "You think I can see them?"

Wrath peers down at the kid. I literally have no idea which direction this will go. For all I know, he could turn into the monster and scare the crap out of Gabe.

But then the shadows pull in closer and take shape.

Gabe's mouth drops open, his eyes glinting with excitement.

My belly warms with a feeling I can't name.

"Tell me, Gabriel," Wrath says, "do you like roller coasters?"

"Oh sure. Me and my friends go to the boardwalk all the time to ride the coaster there. I like to fly, man."

Lisa clears her throat loudly.

"I mean, sir. Mr. Demon King."

The norrow bleed together, then flow around Wrath like a wave. They perfume the air with that primordial scent, like chilly air and rich spices.

Then they dart forward, taking hold of Gabe and lifting him off his feet.

"Whoa!" Gabe yells.

The darkness tosses him in the air and he bellows with laughter as he comes back down only for the darkness to catch him again.

Lisa clutches at her chest, muttering what sounds like a prayer beneath her breath.

Wrath's darkness tosses Gabe again, then spins him around, then dangles him by his ankle.

Gabe roars with laughter the entire time.

I steal a glance at Wrath and find him fighting a smile. The connection between us warms and the warmth flows to me, catching me off guard.

Wrath's eyes dart to me.

Gabe falls through the air, screeching. Rhys hurries beneath him, arms spread out to catch Gabe, but the darkness swoops in at the last second, gently setting him to his feet.

"Holy shit," Gabe says again.

"Gabriel Luis!" Lisa scolds.

"Can you do that again? Please? That was awesome!"

"That's enough for tonight." Rhys ferries the kid toward the door. "Before you give your mother a heart attack."

"Awww, come on, old man."

Emery laughs at the perceived insult, even though technically Rhys *is* an old man. I'm in a room surrounded by old people.

"Thank you, Lisa." Rhys gives the woman a squeeze on the shoulder. "That'll be all for tonight."

As they leave, I hear Lisa castigating the kid, but he's not having any of it. "But Ma! Didn't you see that? It was awesome! Wait till I tell the boys the Demon King threw me around the room with his dark magic!"

Their voices fade away.

I look back to Wrath and find his eyes squarely on me.

The connection thrums again. Something is bothering him. Some emotion that he's trying really hard to bury.

I want to go to him, desperate to reassure him, even though I don't know what he needs reassurance from. But before I can, a guy comes hustling into the room, a backwards baseball cap taming dirty blond hair.

"What is it, Cole?" Rhys asks.

"There's been another attack." Cole's eyes land on Wrath. "And they're blaming him for it."

Wrath bristles but says nothing.

Dane comes in around Cole and grabs a remote. Pressing a button, two panels retract in front of us revealing a giant flat screen TV hidden in the wall. When the screen brightens, Dane flicks to the channel and Grand Central Station comes into view.

People are screaming and flooding from the main doors as darkness ribbons around them.

My stomach drops.

A news anchor ducks and then the camera jostles, the image bouncing.

"Go. Go!" the newsman says.

Darkness shoots behind him.

"It's the Demon King!" someone yells.

The giant arched window that stands over the entrance shatters and glass explodes outward. More screams fill the air.

"Is this live?" I ask and look over at Wrath, suspicious of what he was doing while he was gone.

"Yeah, it's live," Dane answers and I expel a breath of relief.

Wrath frowns at me and I can feel his annoyance echo back to me. "You think I'd do something like this?"

"I don't know," I admit. "You are a villain after all."

"Attacking people in a train station is not only callow at best, but it's also beneath me."

"Damn," Dane says. "The Demon King has standards when it comes to his villainy."

Wrath scowls at the vampire but lets it rest.

Rhys snaps his fingers at Cole and says, "Check on Last Vale. Take a few of the sentinels with you."

Before I can ask what any of that means, Wrath says, "This reeks of Chaos. He's baiting me."

"Then we should do something about it," I say.

There's pandemonium on the screen as the ground rocks and the cameraman loses his footing.

"They think it's you. If you show up to stop him, they'll know you're not the bad guy."

"But I am, *dieva*. I am the villain, as you keep reminding me."

"This isn't a time to be petty."

"Wrath," Rhys says. "If you have the power to stop this, I'll ask you kindly to do so."

Fear flashes through our connection, burning and bright. I inhale sharply and Wrath's attention shifts back to me, his brow furrowing.

He's afraid of facing his brother.

He has so little power left to lose.

"I'll go," I say, taking myself by surprise.

The truth is, I'm a little worried about him too. This is my fault. I'm the reason Chaos is here causing all of this. I'm the reason why Wrath lost part of the triad.

I can fix this. Somehow. I have to do something.

"You will not leave this house," Wrath says, squaring against me. "If you faced my brother, you would lose."

"Why?" I wave my hand in his general direction. "Because I'm not seven feet tall and all bristling muscle?"

"Bristling muscle?" Dane says behind me. "And I doubt he's over six-five."

"I have power, you know." The *animus* comes to me easily, answering my call.

Emery sucks in a breath and Rhys shifts in front of her, shielding her with his body.

Bright, fiery light shines around the room.

I'm suddenly flush with warmth.

I am the *animus*. The power is mine. I can do with it as I please and—

Wrath disappears with a snap of air. I sense him behind me before I can turn to meet him, and that fraction of a second costs me.

He grabs me by the neck and kicks my feet out from beneath me. I'm suddenly blinking at the ceiling and falling fast for the floor.

He catches me before I hit.

Just like Gabe.

I'm a defenseless child next to him.

The power flickers out of me like a spent filament and I'm left with nothing to fight with.

"You won't go up against my brother," he says above me, his face all hard lines and fury. "You don't know the first thing about fighting, let alone controlling your power. You would lose and if he hurt you—" He grits his teeth, cutting himself off.

Pain shoots through the connection. Real and visceral and he tries to tamp it down, but he's not quick enough.

There is nothing we can hide from one another now.

Did he know this would happen when he decided to bind me to him?

I don't think he did. This will be a weakness in his eyes and the Demon King would never choose vulnerability.

"You will not engage with him," he says and winds his arm around my waist, pulling me to my feet.

"So teach me."

"Teach you?"

"Yes. How to use this power. You had it for several hundred years. If anyone knows how to use it, it's you."

He regards me with narrowed eyes. I suppose the old him is thinking anyone having control of the *animus* other than him is a very bad idea. But he'll never have it back. It will always be mine.

Be me.

"I should know how to use it," I try again. "I'm bound to you. I'll always be a target. Not teaching me is a liability at this point."

"She has an excellent point," Rhys says.

A growl rumbles in Wrath's chest as he sends a scathing look at the vampire, but Rhys holds his ground.

I cross my arms over my chest. "Say yes."

He mulls it over, then, "Fine."

"Yes!"

He growls at me. "This is no victory, *dieva*."

"Oh, I beg to differ."

"You'll change your mind soon enough." He tightens his hold on me, draws me into him and then says to Rhys over top of my head, "My brother has one weakness: fire. That information is yours to do with as you please, but I'll not be getting in the middle of it. Not yet anyway."

The air crackles. I know by now what that means.

"Where are we going?"

Wrath peers down at me. "You've requested that I teach you how to fight. Who am I to pass up an opportunity to put you in your place?"

CHAPTER
NINE

Wrath's darkness rips us from Rhys's house. I feel that familiar sensation of being pulled and twisted and popped from one dimension to another and when we reappear, I find us in a training room in what appears to be the castle. There is an entire wall of weapons displayed on a peg rack. Swords and axes, scythes and spears.

My stomach sinks.

What the hell have I gotten myself into?

"Lauren," he yells as he walks over to the weapons.

Since Lauren doesn't have the ability to travel through the sub-dimension, we have to wait for her to make her way to us.

I think it takes her five minutes at least. She looks from Wrath to me and then to the sword in his hand. "Our little *animus* wants to learn how to fight and you're going to fight her."

Lauren's mouth curves into a sinister smile. "About fucking time I get to slit your throat."

Wrath tosses her the sword and she catches it by the hilt easily.

"Where's my weapon?" I ask.

"You don't get one," Wrath says.

"You must be joking."

"Do I joke, *dieva*?"

No. No he doesn't.

"If she cuts me, she cuts you," I point out. "Is that really what you want?"

"No. It is the opposite of what I want." He circles us. "You should do everything in your power to keep your skin intact. Do you understand me?"

I huff out a breath. "I wanted to be taught. Not thrown into hand-to-hand combat with a demon."

Lauren pulls off her t-shirt. She's wearing a black sports bra and black Lululemon pants. Almost like she's been ready for this moment the entire time.

Her demon mark cuts across her chest and arches over her shoulders. Hers isn't as complex as Wrath's is, but it's still impressive.

Can a person vomit from dread? Because I feel like I want to start hurling. Lauren isn't going to go easy on me. Maybe that's why Wrath is pitting me against her.

"Begin," he says.

Lauren gets into a fighting stance.

Fuck.

She circles me for several seconds, sizing me up. I mirror her movements, trying to keep as much distance between us as I can.

I don't know how to approach a fight. What little I learned in self-defense was, well, self-defense. I know nothing about offense.

So I guess the best thing to do is wait for her to—

Lauren charges at me. I yelp and dart away.

"*Dieva*," Wrath warns.

Lauren slices with the blade. I barely get out of the way before losing a chunk of hair from my head.

I dance back and Lauren advances, the blade cocked back. She swings. I duck. But the move costs me precious concentration and Lauren closes the distance between us, slamming the hilt of the sword up into my jaw.

My teeth crack together and a sharp ache zings through my face, throbbing in my eye sockets. Blood wells in my mouth. Wrath stalks around us and spits blood on the floor.

At least he's suffering with me.

But then his gaze darkens, a warning scowl. The more he suffers, the more I suspect I'll suffer the consequences later.

Lauren steps into me again, swings, the blade catching me across the arm. Searing pain shoots down my body as blood immediately fills the cut, several beads sliding down my bicep.

I have no time to assess how deep it is before Lauren is after me again.

She stabs for my gut. I bow my body, just dodging the hit.

The first flare of anger wakes the *animus* and heat races down my arms.

A flicker of flame burns in my hands, except I don't know what to do with it. Can I shoot fire from my fingers? Send magic arcing through the air?

When I faced off with the soldiers in Riverside Park, I conjured flames from nothing. And with Chaos, the *animus* burned away the norrow like they were nothing more than kindling.

But all of that happened in the heat of the moment. I can't remember the actual mechanism to make it work again.

The only thing I really know how to do is call it.

But once I have it, I don't know what to do with it.

Lauren yells a war cry and comes running at me, the blade poised to impale me.

Come on, *animus*!

Flames roll down my arms and when Lauren gets within a few feet of me, the acrid stench of burning flesh fills the air.

Lauren shrieks and scurries backward as smoke rises from her shoulders and her skin turns blistering red.

She has demon magic at her disposal though and she's healed within seconds.

My own magic slips away.

"Nice try," she says and charges again.

I evade her, try to yank the *animus* back up, but the power is being a stubborn bitch and nothing comes to my call.

"Stop thinking about it as separate from you, *dieva*," Wrath says. "It is you and you are it."

Lauren clenches her teeth, rolls her wrist so the blade swipes in an X in front of her body, then comes at me again using fancy footwork to get in beneath my guard. The blade catches me across the chest, cutting through shirt and skin. It happens so fast that the pain comes seconds later.

I shove Lauren back.

"This is stupid," I tell Wrath. "Teach me how to use the *animus* so we can stop Chaos."

"That's one of your problems," he tells me, crossing his arms over his chest. "You're too impatient."

"I've waited long enough, haven't I?"

Lauren ignores our banter and keeps on fighting. She slices through the air, I dodge, then kick out with my foot. The blow makes her knee buckle and she goes down to the floor.

"Use the power," Wrath orders. "Finish the fight."

But when I reach for it, it isn't there. "I can't."

"Why not?"

"I don't know. It's like trying to catch water."

"What brings it out when you do use it?"

I lick my lips, keep my eyes on Lauren as she climbs to her

feet. Sweat is starting to bead on her forehead, so at least she isn't indefatigable.

"*Dieva*," Wrath coaxes.

"Rage, mostly," I answer. "When it comes to me, it's usually out of rage."

"Rage burns quickly," he says. "It's not kindling, it's gasoline. If you want to control it, stop letting it control you."

"I'm not."

"You are." He stalks to the weapon wall. I split my attention between him and Lauren. Big mistake.

Lauren comes at me with the sword, swiping through the air just as Wrath pulls a dagger from the weapons wall and sends it sailing toward me.

The blade glances off my cheek and the pain of the cut burns through my face just as Lauren reaches me and slices through my thigh with her sword.

The *animus* roars to life as white stars blink in my eyes. The pain is overwhelming, nauseating.

"Control it," Wrath says. "Don't let it get away from you." Lauren spins and comes at me with her fist this time just as Wrath grabs another dagger from the wall, cocks his arm back, and throws it.

I am the *animus*.

I shouldn't have to think about using it.

I just can.

I will.

Time slows. I take several settling breaths and anchor myself in my body.

The blade comes sailing right for my throat. The *animus* blooms excitedly at my core.

Without thinking, I snatch the dagger from the air and spin around, sinking the blade into Lauren's shoulder. The fire burns around me, blistering the skin down Lauren's arms, charring it along her collarbone.

She screams, drops to the ground, shaking and crying.

And just when I think I've won—

Wrath slams into me from behind and I go down, pain jolting through my knees. He's on me again in a second, hand wrapped in my hair, yanking my head back. A blade is suddenly at my throat.

"Never let your guard down." His voice is rough at my ear. The blade scrapes painfully against my skin.

"Okay," I say. "I won't."

He lets me go and I lurch to my feet.

"Call it again," he says.

I'm covered in sweat and blood is drying at my wounds, but I put all of it out of my head and focus on the breath in my lungs, the beat of my heart in my ears.

I am not angry. I won't let it control me. For once, I give up the control entirely, letting the power run through me like water instead of me trying to corral it, grip it in my hands.

At first there's nothing and the anxiety at being incapable swims to the surface.

Another deep breath.

Just let go.

The room burns bright orange with a resounding WHUMP.

Wrath circles in front of me and I can see the reflection of the power in his irises.

"Good," he says and tosses another blade up the air and uses his dark magic to shoot it across the room at me.

Sharp awareness takes over me and I can see the blade clearly, can snatch it from the air as if it were a feather caught in a lazy wind.

Once the hilt is in my hand, I spin and throw the dagger back at Wrath. His darkness deflects it, but then he disappears and I turn, focusing on nothing but the here and now, the needling along my back.

I whirl around. He slams into me, but I spin with him and use his own move against him. I kick his feet out from beneath him, slamming him to the floor and quickly climb over top of him, settling over his waist.

Smiling like a maniac, I lord over him. I'm breathing heavily, but new energy wells in my veins.

I'm giddy and a little drunk on power.

"Am I done?" Lauren asks as she slowly climbs to her feet.

Wrath doesn't even look at her. "You're dismissed."

With a grumble, she shuffles to the door and leaves us.

"Well done, *dieva*," Wrath says.

His words are potent, but the pride that thrums through our connection means more.

I can feel him so acutely and my belly soars because of it.

"Thank you," I say.

"You still have a lot of learning to do, but perhaps there's hope for you after all."

I roll my eyes. "You're such an asshole."

Without warning, he grabs me by the waist and rolls me to my back so it's his body covering mine. "Never let your guard down," he warns again, his mouth now inches from mine.

"Yes, daddy."

He grumbles, low and deep in his chest, then gets to his feet and offers me his hand. "You need a shower."

"Speak for yourself."

He wraps his arm around me, sending butterflies charging across my belly, and yanks us to his massive bathroom. Grabbing the hem of my shirt, he peels it none too carefully from my body, the material now glued to the wounds by dried blood. Instinct has me pulling away, anticipating the pain, but there is none.

"Sit," he says and nods at the closed toilet seat. I do as commanded. Using a wet rag, he cleans the wound on my arm, but once the blood is gone, we find the skin intact, not a wound in sight. We find the same on my cheek, on my thigh, and across my chest.

"You're healing quicker." There's a troubled look on his face.

"That's a good thing. The quicker I heal, the less you suffer."

"Mmm," he says and tosses the rag to the sink. "Undress. Get in the shower."

He doesn't have to tell me twice. I may have healed, but my body is still aching and I know the hot water will feel good.

Naked, I step into the stall and turn on the hot water, letting it bead on my skin, soak my hair.

A second later, Wrath is naked and beside me.

"Turn around," he orders.

I turn and face the showerhead.

He takes shampoo in his hands and works it through the tangle of my hair. His fingers on my scalp are almost orgasmic and I have to put my hands on the tiled wall just to keep myself upright.

Suds trail down my back, down my ass. Once he's lathered me up, I turn and rinse out the soap, eyes closed against the hot spray.

When I open them again, Wrath is staring at me, his own gaze crimson red in the murky light of the all-black shower.

His bare chest is rising and falling in a rhythm that spells agitation and the connection beats with curiosity.

"What is it?" I ask.

"Why aren't you afraid of me?"

The question catches me off guard.

"I am afraid of you," I admit.

"No, you're not. I wanted to believe you used your stubbornness to hide your fear, but now with the connection, I know the truth. You're *not* afraid of me. Not like you should be. From the moment I first met you, you refused to bend to me."

"Why does it bother you so much?" I ask, turning it around on him.

"Answer the question, *dieva*."

I lean against the shower wall, giving him the showerhead. He steps beneath it, puts his face into the spray, scrubs away the sweat.

"If you want the truth," I say, "I don't know what the answer is. Maybe it was the *animus*, maybe it recognized you."

"You have to stop talking about it like it's separate from you." He turns sideways and the water glances off his broad shoulder, trails down the cut of his bicep, down the nip of his waist.

I don't want to look down at his cock, because I know what the sight of his nakedness will do to me and it doesn't feel like the right time for that.

"Your turn," I say and reach over, using my thumb to rub off a smudge of blood along his jaw. He lets me do it. Doesn't flinch.

The air nearly vibrates between us, the connection wobbling on its axis if it had one.

"What was the question?" he asks on a rasp.

"Why does it bother you so much that I'm not afraid of you? Is it just the power and the control?"

He comes closer, pinning me into the corner of the shower.

"I thought it was your disobedience."

I smirk.

"But now I realize it's something else."

"Tell me."

The water circles the drain, beading on the tiled wall as steam fills the space that we don't occupy.

"You are an enigma and I've always hated mysteries. But

more than that, I don't recognize myself when I'm with you."

He's more terrified of me than I am of him.

I am sure of that because I can feel it rippling through our connection.

"Is that why you left Rhys's house in a hurry earlier? I felt... when we...*you*—"

Love.

That's what I felt.

Love.

He licks his lip, then rakes his teeth over it, avoiding my eyes and I realize I've overstepped. His walls are coming back up.

I quickly change subjects. "Where did you go anyway, when you left?"

"To the place I go to when I need to breathe."

"Which is where?" I'm more curious for this detail than I have been for others before it and I'm glad to keep him talking.

"Finish up and I'll show you."

"Really? Promise?"

"I promise, *dieva*." A smirk comes to his sensual mouth.

I rinse out the rest of my hair and scrub the blood from my body. He finishes before me, towels off and dresses in his dark jeans, a black t-shirt and the black coat I first saw him in, in the alley behind Collie's Tea Shop. The collar stands rigid around his pale face.

I dress in clothes I find hanging in a section in his closet. A section that appears to be just for me.

"Wear a jacket," he instructs me. There's a black bomber jacket in the closet, so I slip into it.

"Ready?" he asks and holds out his hand.

I'm giddy with anticipation. Where does the Demon King go to get away? He can literally go anywhere in the world.

"Ready."

He grabs hold of me and pulls us away.

CHAPTER

TEN

WE REAPPEAR UNDER A TWILIGHT SKY. THE AIR IS CHILLED AND goosebumps lift on my arms despite the coat. Wind cuts across the foreign landscape and sand skitters over my shoes. It's the only sound save for the rasp of clothing and the rapid beating of my heart.

Wrath lets me go and I stumble back as the ground shifts easily beneath me.

It's sand. All of it is sand.

"Where are we?" I spin a circle, my eyes adjusting to the darkness. There's nothing but rolling sand dunes as far as the eye can see with a row of dark mountains in the distance. It's so quiet, so vast, it feels like another world.

"White Sands National Park in New Mexico," he tells me.

For all of the traveling I've done with my mother, I've only been to a desert once. Mom typically prefers lush landscapes like Scotland or Iceland, full of color and texture and depth.

"Deserts are temperamental," she told me on our way to the Mojave when I was just eight years old. "I'm not full of much hope for this shoot, but I go where they pay me."

It was blisteringly hot. Not hot like Florida where the air

sticks to your skin. Hot like you've opened the oven door and stood right in front of it, letting the heat bake your skin from your bones.

I was excited about seeing the desert that day with Mom only because I'd never been and I'd heard that deserts were their own sort of magic.

After that shoot, I hated deserts as much as she did. I was sunburnt despite the layers and layers of sunscreen and the wide-brimmed hat and the sunglasses. "I'm never ever going to another desert," I told her that night while she rubbed cold aloe on my skin.

"Don't worry, baby," she'd said. "I'll die before I go to another."

But standing on a dune of white sand with the Demon King beside me, I have to eat my words.

This desert is much different than the Mojave and I realize I unfairly judged deserts based only on one and only beneath the blistering sun.

This desert at night is otherworldly.

Above me, the Milky Way splits the dark sky nearly in two. There are so many stars in the sky, I get dizzy just looking up.

"This is beautiful."

It's so quiet here, my whispers sound like a shout.

"Your world does have its moments of searing beauty."

I glance over at Wrath, but he's not looking at the sky.

He's looking at me.

My stomach drops, my heart beats a little harder.

The connection between us thrums and this time, he doesn't try to hide it. More and more, he gives and gives and I am desperate to have it.

To have him.

"How often do you come here?" I ask.

"Often enough."

91

"It's lonely, isn't it?"

He turns away from me, his head bent toward the sky. His footsteps follow the sharp edge of a dune, breaking it beneath each step. "I'm used to being alone."

I follow him, walking in the imprints of his boots. "I am too."

He glances at me over a shoulder. A gust of wind rumples his hair and I have to fight the urge to reach across the space between us and run my fingers through it, watch him bend to my touch.

"You are surrounded by people who love you," he says.

"Yeah, that's true, but..." I trail off, trying to figure out how to put it into words. "My mother was a good mother, but because I acted like I didn't need her, she pretended she wasn't needed."

"Did you?" His eyes flicker red in the light. "Need her?"

A wave of emotion takes hold in my chest, squeezing the air from my lungs. "Maybe. Yes. Sometimes I did."

He turns away, keeps walking.

"Have you ever needed someone?" I ask.

"Of course."

"When?"

"I needed you," he admits.

"That's not what I meant."

"Isn't it?" He comes to a halt and I lurch to a stop behind him, the ground shifting beneath me. "Do you want to hear something truly fucked up?"

"Oh yes. Please go on. I like fucked up things."

He's quiet for a handful of seconds and I think it's because he's considering what to say and how to say it, which only builds my eagerness to hear it.

"When I lost the *animus*," he starts, "I was desperate to get it back. I missed it like a limb and ached with the absence of it.

When I met you for the first time, that void disappeared and it terrified me." He meets my eyes. "I had forgotten what it was to be whole."

My breathing quickens.

"When you left me again and again...the void yawned open and every second you were gone..." He takes in a breath, the fine lines around his eyes deepening. "Every second you were gone, I missed you."

The breath catches in my throat.

My gaze blurs with tears.

"I thought about you every waking minute. I still do, even when I have you chained to my bed. I can't ever stop thinking about you and I fucking hate it. I hate how the sight of you is burned to memory like hot metal touched to wood, a permanent char mark right here behind my eyes. You are always there." He clenches his teeth, jaw flexing, and turns away from me, speaks to the sky. "I hate that just the scent of you makes me hard. I hate that the sound of your voice makes me want to be gentle.

"But most of all, I hate that when you're quivering beneath me, I feel like I've laid my hands on something that only the gods can touch."

His back is still to me, but I can see him plainly in my mind, the char mark burned to memory. The cut of his jaw, the slope of his nose. The way his Adam's apple sinks when he swallows his frustrations.

He may be a demon, a *king*, but when I love him the most, he is just a man.

I go to him and wind my arms around his waist, hook my hands at his stomach. "I hate you too," I say. He puts his hands on mine, threads his fingers with my fingers.

"I am a man fighting against the wind and you are a gale force, *dieva*. And I don't like being powerless."

My belly is immediately soaring.

I move around him so we're facing each other. His expression is hard-edged, wary.

I feel it too, that inescapable tug at the center of me, even before we were bound. We were always supposed to come together. I am the *animus* and he is the king.

I reach up on tiptoes to kiss him.

He's stiff at first.

We're two lonely creatures unaccustomed to needing someone else, to being needed.

And worse, trusting them.

"No more games," I tell him as his eyes slip closed, as his hands slide to my waist, coaxing a moan to escape me. "I made my decision. I bound myself to you and I plan to embrace it, all of it. I don't ever want you to feel powerless because of me."

"It's too late for that." His mouth comes down on mine, hard. I breathe out through my nose as the kiss deepens, as his hands sink to my ass and he drives me against his hard cock.

I want to sink into him. I want to disappear into him and the pleasure of fucking and nothing more. None of the complications of our relationship and the position we find ourselves in.

Reaching between us, I grope him over his jeans and he growls into my mouth, nipping at my lip. A hiss comes out of me and he swallows it up, his hand possessive on the back of my head.

I fumble with the button on his jeans and when I finally get it open, he's straining against the material of his boxer briefs.

I try to pull him out, but the sand shifts beneath me and I lose my footing.

But his darkness catches me before I topple over. It crests into a wave around me, holding me tightly.

And in an instant, Wrath is on top of me, his darkness suspending us mid-air.

I yelp, unaccustomed to being weightless.

The darkness ebbs and flows, lifting us higher, and I flail against it, fighting it.

"Give in to me, *dieva*," he says. "Surrender to me."

The sand dunes are far below us now and we're so high in the sky, I swear I could reach out and touch the moon.

"Do you trust me?" he asks as his eyes brighten, more crimson than grey.

Do I? I don't know that I've fully given in to anyone in my entire life. I've always been alone because I've chosen to be alone, because it's always easier to rely only on yourself.

When you only rely on yourself, no one can disappoint you.

Or betray you.

The darkness steals my shirt, then my pants, leaving me in a matching set of black lace underthings. Wrath's deft fingers slip in beneath the band of my bra, teasing at the sensitive underside of my breast. My nipple peaks, aches for him.

I hang my head back and close my eyes. Maybe if I don't look at the sky or the ground beneath us, I can give in to the pleasure of my body and not the terror.

"*Dieva?*" he asks.

"Yes," I say, a little breathless. "I trust you."

He relieves us of the rest of our clothes and they flutter to the sand dunes twenty feet below.

I make the mistake of looking down and choke on a yelp, but Wrath is clever about distracting me. His hands trail down, right under my ass so that his fingers hit on my inner thighs and coax me open for him.

The head of his cock nestles at my opening and I whimper, desperate for him to be inside of me.

His mouth trails down the side of my jaw, down the curve of

my neck. He nips at me, I jolt, and he tightens his hold on me as the darkness ribbons around us, holding us aloft.

He continues his slow, tortuous descent of his mouth and I arch into him, begging him to take my nipple in his mouth. And when he finally does, I mewl beneath him. We may be rising to the stars, but I'm descending into the pleasure of his mouth.

Tongue teasing at me, he brings me to a peak and then bites at me, sucks me back into his mouth, then eases the sting with a slide of his tongue.

His cock presses forward and I rock my hips up, trying to sink him deeper.

The darkness pivots, righting us, and Wrath settles me on his hips and coaxes my legs around him. I use his body as leverage and try to drive him into me.

But he holds himself steady.

"I will always control your pleasure, *dieva*."

I moan into him, a little mindless for more.

"Not even the *animus* can take that from me."

I rock against him again, but he hooks his hands beneath my thighs and lifts me off of him, stealing the heat of his cock from my opening.

I moan at the loss.

"Are you always going to torture and tease me and make me beg?"

"Yes," he admits and slides his shaft up my wetness, the head of his cock hitting my clit. He drags back again, then up, back and up.

The sensation steals the breath from my lungs and I gasp to get it back.

"Then please fuck me."

"Try that again."

"Please fuck me, my king."

"Good girl."

I'll beg for it all day long. This part of myself I can give him. I can give up control when he's fucking me because when he's fucking me, I feel whole.

He sinks inside of me, forcing a moan from my lips.

The darkness tightens arounds us, surrounds us on all sides save for above where the Milky Way glitters and glows.

Wrath picks up his rhythm, driving into me. He's harder than he's ever been and I can feel every ridge of him inside of me.

"Fuck, *dieva*," he says, in and out, filling me up.

The pleasure builds.

I hang my head back and the stars blur into bright white lines.

Wrath pinches my nipple between two fingers, sending a jolt of pain through me and then quickly covers it with his mouth, stopping the pain with a caress of his tongue.

"You will always be mine," he says.

"Yes."

"And I will always worship you if you'll let me."

Worship me. Reign. The Bright Goddess.

It's almost like the moon is taunting me from the sky.

Wrath drives into me harder, and I cream around him as he brings me closer and closer to the brink.

The darkness envelops us and it caresses against my skin like silk.

My nerves are lit up like lightning. Every sensation is like a revolution, like a star being born.

"Come for me, *dieva*," he says. "I want to feel that tight pussy pulse around my cock."

He shifts us, so that I'm bouncing on his shaft, my arms around his neck.

Warmth spreads through me and when I open my eyes, a bright golden light is filling the dark cloud around us. It sends a soft flow across Wrath's sharp face, driving away his shadows.

"I don't know if I can," I say. I'm close, but it's all so much, too much.

"It wasn't a request." He flips me over and the darkness nestles me into its dark waves. Wrath drives back into me, buries himself to the hilt. His hand comes to the column of my neck, fingers pressing hard into me.

"Come for me, *dieva*. That's an order."

His other hand sinks between my legs, presses against my mound.

I'm suddenly squirming beneath him, desperate for friction as my clit throbs and my body pulses for release.

He swirls two fingers against me, pulling the orgasm closer and closer and—

I cry out. The pleasure rushes in.

I quiver beneath him as he nestles against my ass, cock buried so deep, it almost hurts.

He pulls out, slams back in, cups me as I ride through the wave of the orgasm, then flicks my clit again, causing me to shudder.

"Fuck," I breathe out, the golden glow intensifying in our nest of darkness.

Wrath pounds harder, punishing my pussy until he slams in deep and fills me up.

His fingers press at my throat, stealing some of the air from my lungs. I hold my breath as he throbs inside of me.

As my body blinks through the aftershocks, Wrath slides out several inches, then slides back in, slow and torturous. His grip on my throat loosens and he finally lets me curl into myself, curl into him.

The darkness undulates, then holds us like a black cloud and Wrath wraps his arms around me.

We lay there for the longest time, the bright sky above us, the darkness below. We're suspended in a dark daydream where none of the shit can reach us.

Soon I find myself drifting off to sleep.

"*Dieva*." His voice is hoarse at my ear.

"Hmm?"

His fingers trail through my hair and it sends a shiver down my spine.

"I can't love you the way you deserve to be loved."

I open my eyes. Moonlight skims the dark clouds with pale silver light.

I know he means it as a warning.

We haven't had this conversation yet. We haven't been brave enough to look it in the eye, give it a name.

But that is what we have, isn't it? Some kind of love, as twisted as it may be.

"Just love me how you can," I tell him.

The moonlight disappears. Wrath pulls us through the sub-dimension back to his bed. He lays me gently on the sheets, pulls the blanket around me as I tremble.

I'm so warm and I feel so safe.

We can figure this out.

I know we can.

But nestled in his arms, as I descend into sleep, I hear him whisper, "But will that be enough?"

CHAPTER
ELEVEN

I wake to Lauren peering down at me.

I shriek. Wrath holds me still, his face still buried in my neck, in my hair. "This better be important," he says behind me.

Sunlight is pouring in around the partially opened drapes. I have no idea what time it is, but I've become a creature of the night. It could very well be two in the afternoon.

"Kat is here and she's brought you a present."

Though I can't see Wrath, I sense his curiosity through the connection. "Don't leave me in suspense."

"Apparently they caught someone trying to sneak into Last Vale. They think he's one of Chaos's men. Kat brought the trespasser to you."

Wrath disentangles himself from me and collapses on his back. "I'll be there in a minute."

Lauren nods and leaves.

I suppose when you're the one in charge, there is no such thing as a day off.

"What's Last Vale?" I ask. "Rhys said something about it last night too."

"It's a hidden town in Saint Sabine that Rhys founded a long time ago. It's to be a safe haven for the supernatural."

"Why would this guy want to go there?"

"There's a powerful ley line that runs beneath it. The same ley line that Ciri used to pull me to your world."

I sit up. "Do you think Chaos is trying to open a portal?"

"It's certainly possible. I wouldn't put it past him." He throws the sheet and the duvet back and slides from the bed. I take a minute to appreciate the view of him walking away, his bare ass, the way his back dimples, all muscle and bone.

"Stop leering at me."

"I'm not. I'm appreciating what's mine."

He grumbles as he disappears into the closet. "Clever little girl."

I sigh and collapse back against the pillows that smell like him.

"You should dress as well," he calls out to me. "I'd like you by my side."

A thrill buzzes through me. "Really?"

He comes out dressed in his usual—black jeans, black t-shirt, black boots. He is a dark vision. He runs his hand through his equally dark hair, raking it back. Even though we showered last night, his hair is somehow perfectly coiffed in that roguish, careless way only someone like him can manage.

"From now on," he says, "I want you always by my side."

It sounds perfunctory, cold, but the connection doesn't lie —this isn't about appearances. He doesn't want to be without me.

It's been so long since I've had an obsessive crush that I forgot what it felt like to be so wound up in someone that you couldn't imagine walking away from them.

I can't call this a crush, though. This is something else. Something deeper.

But the overwhelming need is still there, echoing back to each other through the vein of energy that runs between us.

I don't even have to say anything. He already knows.

I'll be there. I'll stay by his side.

"Get dressed," he orders and waits for me on the balcony.

I throw on the first thing I see—a white t-shirt, black skinny jeans. I find a row of shoes on a shelf on the bottom of my section in the closet. Tennis shoes, flats, stilettos, and several pairs of booties.

I go with a pair of black booties.

In the bathroom, I rake my hand through my hair, but mine is flat and limp, and doesn't do that roguish wave like Wrath's does. Maybe when this is all over, I'll make a hair appointment. I deserve a treat-yourself day after marrying a demon and battling his demon brother.

Back in the bedroom, Wrath turns away from the balcony. Even though I'm in nothing more than jeans and a t-shirt, he drinks in the sight of me like I've donned a princess dress, hair curled and pinned.

My chest warms.

He comes over, hooks his arm around me and plants a kiss on my mouth, his hand sinking to my ass. A flare of desire wells at my core and Wrath tsk-tsks.

"Sorry," I say, even though I'm not.

"Business first, fucking second."

"Shouldn't that be the other way around?"

"Not when you're king and queen."

I pout up at him and he smiles easily, his gray eyes glittering. "I may not know how to properly love you, *dieva*, but I do know how to fuck you. I'll make it up to you."

"Promise?"

"Always."

He pulls us from the bedroom and deposits us in a distant hallway where voices carry out from an unmarked room.

Inside, we find Kat and Lauren with a man tied to a chair.

There are no windows in the room and only one door. There's no furniture save for the chair.

Blood is crusted along the man's jaw and his left eye is turning a bruised shade of violet.

"I checked him for location charms," Kat says. "And bound him so no one can use him for a location spell."

Wrath nods his approval.

The guy is veering back and forth between sobbing and laughter. Tears stream down his face and his eyes are wide open, giving him a crazed look.

"It doesn't matter," he says.

Wrath stalks over, circles the guy slowly. The guy fights at the ropes binding him, causing the chair to creak, the ropes to groan.

"Did Chaos send you?" Wrath asks.

The guy laughs and the laughter descends into sobs. He's not much older than me. He might have been a college student or an office drone. There's nothing special about him. Maybe working for a demon is the height of his potential.

"You'll never stop him," the guy says.

"Stop him from doing what?" Wrath asks.

The guy spits on the floor just missing Wrath's boot. "Stealing your girl and your throne."

Wrath bristles. The connection vibrates and I want to crawl out of my skin. I'm not made for interrogation, it would seem.

"What were you doing in Last Vale?" Kat asks.

"Looking for the portal."

Wrath and Kat glance at each other. "Did he find it?" Wrath asks her.

"Not as far as we know. He was just outside the city."

"He couldn't have opened it without a traveler," Lauren says. "Right?"

"There are other ways to get through," Kat answers. "None of them easy though."

Something is troubling Wrath.

"What are you thinking?" I ask him.

"Chaos has the *oculus* and your government on his side. A billion-dollar military at his disposal. I don't know why he'd go to the trouble of opening a gate when it's not soldiers he needs."

The man goes quiet and winces from pain as he shifts in the chair.

"Something else is wrong," Wrath says. "A problem he can't solve." Wrath turns his attention back to the prisoner. "The question is, do you know?"

The man shakes his head, tears dripping from his face. "I don't. I don't know anything."

"If you don't know anything, then what good are you?"

A bead of bloodlust takes hold of Wrath and it wells up inside of me. He's growing impatient and eager for violence. It almost makes my head spin, how quickly he's gone from smiling at me in the bedroom to murder.

"What's your name?" I ask, trying to defuse the tension.

"Zach."

"Zach, if you help us, maybe we can help you."

I get a sharp poke of disapproval through the connection. Wrath scowls at me.

"I don't know anything," he says again. "I swear it. I..." He grimaces. "Sorry. I..." He grits his teeth, tendons standing out in his neck from the strain.

"Zach," I try again, "tell us every little detail you might know. Even if it seems insignificant. Can you do that?"

"I can't." He descends into madness again and hangs his head back and laughs.

"What is wrong with him?" I ask. "This doesn't seem normal."

"It isn't. This is what happens when you either don't have the power or the knowledge to use the *oculus* on someone."

The guy turns to crying again, snot running down his nose. "I can't do it. You can't stop him." He laugh-cries. "Please help me."

"This is a waste of time." Cold impatience reverberates through our connection. Wrath stalks forward.

"Wait!"

He puts his hands on either side of Zach's head and gives him a violent twist.

The sound of bones cracking makes my stomach see-saw. Zach's body goes limp, his head turned at an unnatural angle.

I clamp my hand over my mouth.

Wrath points at Lauren. "Clean this up." Then he stalks from the room.

I hurry after him, still queasy. "Why did you do that?"

"He was useless and his mind was scrambled."

I race ahead, cutting him off.

"He was a human being."

Wrath frowns down at me. "And?"

"And. And! He deserved...something..."

"He was an enemy and he needed to be dealt with. That is how this goes."

"No. I don't want that to be the way we deal with problems. That isn't—"

He looks away from me, his gaze going distant as if he's hearing something I can't.

"What is it?"

Horror washes over his face. He reaches out for me, but an

explosion rocks the floor as debris fills the air. I'm tossed backward and slam into the wall. All of the breath is knocked from my lungs and I slink down to the floor gasping.

There's shouting and yelling. Dust plumes around me while flames grow in the background.

I can taste sulphur in the back of my throat.

Another explosion goes off and the heat intensifies.

I still can't breathe. Everything hurts. I think I broke a rib, maybe punctured a lung.

"*Dieva!*" Wrath shouts.

"I'm here," I try to say, but my voice is barely more than a whisper.

At the other end of the hall, a gun lets out a pop-pop and bullets whiz by.

More shouting fills the halls. Another bomb, then another and the castle rocks on its foundation. Someone screams.

I'm disoriented. My head is ringing. I should run. I should do something, right?

I need to get out of the smoke, get fresh air, clear my lungs so I can think straight.

Arm clutched over my body trying to keep the pain at bay, I drag my hand along the stone wall until I find the next break in the hall and go right, and finally stumble into an exterior door. I burst outside, drag in a breath.

When the dust clears from my eyes, I realize I'm not alone in the back garden.

And worse, it's someone I recognize.

Ryder, the leader of the Men Against Wrath. And standing beside him is Tom, the man from the farmhouse down the road, the very same man I was dumb enough to inform of the castle. The Demon King's castle. The one hidden by magic unless you know where to look.

Fucking hell.

I'm such a fucking idiot!

"Rain!" Tom says and hurries over to me. "Are you okay?"

"What is going on?" I whisper and try to stand upright but my back is killing me and there's a sharp pain in my side that hurts like hell when I take a deep breath.

Ryder stalks over, shoves Tom aside and stabs me in the gut.

A scream claws from my throat. The pain is so intense, I immediately drop where I stand.

The world spins.

"What are you doing?" Tom tries to attend to me, but one of Ryder's men yanks the old man back. "We're supposed to be saving her!"

Taking a length of my hair, Ryder winds it around his knuckles and yanks me to my feet.

My vision goes bright white as the pain overwhelms every nerve in my body.

"Yes, but a little pain can't hurt. Especially when it weakens the Demon King." Ryder smiles at me as he produces another blade.

Somewhere at the other end of our connection, I can feel the Demon King struggling through the mirroring wound while he fights the people swarming the castle's halls.

And with the pain, I can feel his panic.

He can feel me slipping.

There's so much blood. It's just pouring out of me, soaking my shirt, my pants, running down my leg.

"This isn't right," Tom says.

Ryder nods at one of his men. "Percy, escort the old man home. He's done his part."

"I'm sorry, Rain." Tom reaches out for me, but Percy yanks him away. "I didn't know."

A second blade flashes in Ryder's grip and he plunges that one into my shoulder with a swift, downward thrust.

My knees buckle. I let out a pathetic sob as I hit the dirt.

"Chaos said she needed to be alive," one of Ryder's men warns. "We should probably hold back, boss."

Ryder screws up his mouth. "I'm sure she can take it," he says as he twists the blade in my shoulder.

The pain is so intense that my vision blurs on the edges and tears stream down my face. I'm going to vomit. I want to leave my body so I never have to feel this kind of pain ever again.

"Get her up." Ryder stalks away. "Bring her to the car."

Two men hook me through the arms and drag me across the back garden to a waiting SUV in the driveway. I'm tossed into the backseat and fresh pain wends through my body.

Make it stop.

I need to make it stop.

"Burn the place to the ground," Ryder orders before he climbs in behind the wheel and tromps on the gas, tearing us away.

I PASS out in the backseat of the SUV.

I have no idea how long we're on the road.

The next thing I know, I'm waking on a couch in a darkened room and Chaos is sitting in a chair in front of me.

"Hello, Rain," he says.

I lurch awake and pull myself into a sitting position as far away from him as I can.

But as I blink the grogginess from my eyes, I get a good look at him.

He looks like shit.

The tortoiseshell glasses are gone and the whites of his eyes are bloodshot, dark circles marring his skin beneath. His lips are dry and cracked and his skin is so thin and pale, it's almost translucent.

Worse, his veins are turning black.

"What's wrong with you?" I ask.

I just saw him on the news and he didn't look like this. Though I bet there was some magic of TV makeup going on.

"It's the *oculus*." Sirene's voice comes from my left. I find the shape of her in the darkened corner, her arms folded over her chest. "He can't hold on to it."

Chaos grimaces, clearly miffed about this turn of events.

"It's eating away at him from the inside and that little show at the train station only made it worse."

Chaos leans back against the chair and sighs. There is the barest flicker of relief in his eyes as if sitting upright caused him a great deal of pain and discomfort.

"I thought you were stronger?" I turn to Sirene. "You and Ciri had a plan and you manipulated me into joining you. I thought this was your goal."

"This *was* her goal." Chaos rolls his head along the back of the chair so he can glare at the witch. "She and Ciri knew it all along, didn't you? You knew exactly where we'd end up. You knew I was the only one who would have the power and the desire to steal the *oculus* from Wrath." He recenters, looks at me. "She knew I'd steal it, but could never hold it, forcing me to give it to you because I'm certainly not giving it back to my brother." He coughs, grimaces, and blood speckles the corner of his mouth. "I was just a pawn in her game and so are you."

I rise to my feet and Chaos flinches.

He's afraid of me.

"So now what? You attack Wrath's castle using MAW to do it? Ryder is a fucking psychopath, by the way. Then you bring me here and...what? What the fuck do you expect me to do now? And where is Wrath?"

I can still feel him through the connection, so I know he's alive, but he's very far away and I can't tell what state he's in.

What I do feel is *terror* at being separated from me.

Sirene pushes away from the wall and comes over. Her long dirty blonde hair is braided into three tight braids that run along the side of her head. She looks better than Chaos does, but there are fine lines of stress crowing at her eyes.

"When I first held you," Sirene says, "this wailing fat little baby, I thought, 'This is a mistake.' I thought the gods were surely laughing at me because you wouldn't shut up." She comes closer. "It's easy to doubt something when you can't see the shape of it yet."

I frown. "I hate riddles."

Chaos puts his hands on the arms of the chair and uses them as leverage to bring himself to his feet. He winces, grunts, and then takes a long breath once he's standing, chest wheezing.

So much for the mighty Chaos.

I don't know why we were ever afraid of him. I could probably punch him in the balls right now and he'd keel over.

With trembling fingers, he undoes the buttons on his shirt and then pulls it off. He may be withering away, but he's still cut like a fighter. His biceps bulge as he moves, his abs contracting as he tosses the shirt aside.

He hasn't lost muscle mass, but something is very, very wrong with his demon mark.

It's jagged and fading away and there's a raw, festering burn mark over his right collarbone.

That must be the *oculus*.

On Wrath's demon mark, there's a gaping hole at the center of it where I think the *animus* used to be. Now I wear the mark between my shoulder blades.

Chaos puts his hand over his infected wound and grits his teeth together.

"What are you doing?"

He groans.

"Sirene, what is he doing?"

His face turns blue while his eyes glow bright red.

The demon mark moves beneath his skin like slippery ink and then his knees buckle and he hits the floor with a loud thud.

"Sirene!"

"Stand back," she says evenly.

I scurry over to the end of the couch.

The demon mark glows red to match Chaos's eyes.

The hair rises along my arms.

Chaos hangs his head back and roars as the *oculus* leaves his body. And when it's over, he bends forward, breathing heavily. There's a stone clutched in his hand.

It looks distinctly like black volcanic rock, just like from the stories.

Sirene wrenches the stone from him. He knows he can't hold it but it takes considerable effort for him to let it go.

This was supposed to be his silver bullet, the beginning of his brother's end.

Sirene comes over to me. I scurry off the couch, slide along the wall. She follows me, the *oculus* sitting innocently in the palm of her hand, innocent like an unlit bomb.

"What do you plan to do with it now?" I ask.

"What I did with the *animus*."

"Ummm...no." I backpedal. She mirrors me. "Sirene. No."

"Why?"

"Because. It belongs to Wrath—"

"No, it doesn't."

"—and if Chaos isn't strong enough to contain it then neither am I."

"Yes, you are."

"No, I'm not."

I hit the corner of the room and Sirene stops in front of me.

"I'm not taking it."

"You don't have to *take* it," she says. "I'm giving it to you."

"Wrath will never trust me if I have two-thirds of the Demon King's power. I barely know how to control the *animus*, let alone the *oculus*. It'll probably burn me up inside and—"

Sirene tosses the stone into the air.

My eyes track it as it arches above my head.

Without thinking, almost as if of their own accord, my hands snap out and catch the stone before it hits the ground.

Heat races up my arm. Light flares in my field of vision.

Sirene staggers back as I mash myself against the wall, as some unseen force roars through the room.

I'm filled with fire. So much fire. It's like I've touched the sun, like my skin is pulling back from meat and bone, incinerating every fiber of my being.

I can't contain it. I'm not meant for this.

It feels like my insides are being rearranged, my cells reborn, my bones hollowed out and filled with molten lava.

I hang my head back and scream.

CHAPTER

TWELVE

W<small>HEN THE PAIN FINALLY EBBS</small>, I'<small>M ON MY BUTT ON THE FLOOR</small>, <small>BUT AT</small> least I still have eyelids.

Sirene and Chaos peer over top of me. "I told you," Sirene says.

Chaos curses.

"What. The. Fuck." I sit upright and— "Holy shit."

In a blink, I'm on my feet. It's like I've snorted coke and downed a bottle of liquor. Not that I know what it's like to snort drugs. I'm just guessing here.

There is no pain. No aches. I'm full of so much energy, I think I could touch the sky.

I want to run. Fly. Fight. Fuck.

Holy shit.

Holy shit.

Have I finally lost my mind? Maybe Zach wasn't the crazy one. Maybe I've gone mad.

I bring my hands in front of my face. I can see the blood pumping through my veins, the tiny whirls of my fingerprints when I focus on them.

I can hear the birds chirping outside, the worms moving in the earth, and the distant churning of a motor.

"What is this?" Even my voice sounds different, richer, more complex.

"Two-thirds of the Demon King's power," Chaos says begrudgingly.

I pace the room. I can't sit still. "This isn't...how do I...Wrath will... *Why*?" I stop and look at Chaos and Sirene. "Why would you give this to me? I'm not your ally. And I'm bound to the Demon King."

Sirene smirks. "Really? You hold power majority. I think it is *he* who is bound to *you* now."

"No. No no no." I keep pacing. "He's going to kill me. He's never going to believe that I didn't want this. He's going to think it was all part of the plan and—Sirene. Take it back." I hold out my hands. "You need to take it back."

"I can't. I won't."

"Why not?"

Chaos settles himself back into his chair. I can hear the unsteady thrum of his heart. He's not doing well. I don't know how I know it but I do. The mighty demon brother, laid so low by nothing more than his ambition.

"Because," he says, wincing as he looks up at me, "she believes you're the reincarnated goddess Reignyabit and if that's true, the power was always yours. It was always meant to be yours."

CHAPTER
THIRTEEN

I LEAVE THE ROOM. WE'RE IN A STERILE OFFICE BUILDING FROM THE looks of it with prison gray walls and cheap tiled floors and fluorescent lights that buzz above me.

The buzz is so loud it makes me wince.

At the end of the hall, I find a stairwell with a placard that says we're on the second floor.

Sirene comes after me. "Rain, wait."

"Fuck off." I burst into the stairwell, the door's push handle clanking loudly.

Wrath is going to be pissed. How will I explain this one? We had just gotten on solid ground again in our relationship.

Sirene's footsteps echo behind me. "Rain."

"I'm just going to give it back to him," I tell her. "So your plan was stupid and fruitless and it cost Ciri her life."

"Ciri knew what she was doing."

"She wanted to die?"

"She knew she had to."

I snort and the sound boomerangs back to me. "I'm giving it back to him."

"You can't."

"Yes, I can."

"No." She vaults herself over the stair railing and cuts me off at the next landing, her braids flipping over her shoulder. "You're not listening to me. You *can't* give it back to him."

"I'm not a reincarnated goddess. Okay! I know the stories. I read about them in a vampire's library. The dark god and the bright goddess. I know how the story goes. But that's not me. I'm just a girl."

"If you were just a girl, then how can you possibly possess so much power and contain it?" She comes up a step. I go up one more. "Chaos is a demon of royal blood and he nearly died holding on to just one part of the triad."

My throat thickens.

"Now you have two. Tell me, Rain, do you feel like you're dying?"

Fuck.

She comes up another step.

My vision blurs as tears well in my eyes. "This isn't supposed to happen this way."

"Answer the question."

"No, all right? I feel like...like..." I tip my head back, close my eyes, purging a tear. I quickly swipe it away. "I feel bigger," I answer. "Not physically though. Something else. Something *other*."

Not even thinking about it, my senses expand beyond the stairwell. Immediately I can tell there are seven men on the ground floor. Two of them are drinking coffee. The third is drinking cheap whiskey. I know it's cheap because I can smell it.

Ryder's voice cuts through the din. "Fucking bitch bleeds like any other," he's saying. "There's nothing special about her."

One of the others laughs. "I don't know. If she's got a special cunt, I'd like to get a taste of it."

Ryder groans. "She's been fucking that demon for weeks. Tainted cunt isn't my thing."

"Bullshit," someone else says. "Given the opportunity, you'd tie that bitch to a tree and fuck her till she bled."

There's a pause, and then Ryder says, "Yeah, you're right."

They all erupt in laughter.

Sirene regards me with suspicion. "What is it? What are you hearing?"

The otherness at the center of me grows claws and sharp teeth.

I lose my train of thought.

The rage kicks up, familiar and comforting.

Bright golden light fills the stairwell.

"Stop." Sirene puts her hand out and there's a loud WHUMP. The air in front of me ripples and glows and my nose fills with the scent of smoky oak.

This is Sirene's magic. "Not yet," she says.

I blink. "What?"

"You've got the murder face on."

"I...I don't have a murder face."

"You do now."

"I wasn't—"

"You can deal with Ryder soon enough."

I huff and cross my arms over my chest. "What is this, some kind of magical force field?" I poke a finger at the rippling blue light and the air crackles like thin ice before disintegrating into a plume of smoke.

Sirene's mouth drops open.

I wrinkle my nose. I don't think that's how that was supposed to happen.

With an arch of her sharp brow, Sirene says, "Not a goddess, huh?"

"I don't know what that was."

"I'm several hundred years old and one of the most powerful witches in your world *and* mine."

"Hello, hubris."

"No one can dismantle my magic with a poke of their finger."

I worry at my bottom lip, trying to come up with a good excuse. "Maybe you're tired."

She scowls at me.

"Hungry? Stressed?"

"Can I show you something?"

Sirene has never asked me anything before. She's commanded. Begrudgingly tolerated.

Never asked.

"As if I would be stupid enough to go anywhere with you."

"You're the one driving. I promise no tricks."

"I don't have a car. You brought me here."

"Not a car."

It dawns on me what she's jiving toward. "I don't know how to travel through the sub-dimension. At least not on purpose."

"I saw you use it once before. It should be a piece of cake now."

Now that I'm a goddess, apparently.

It's all bullshit.

"Okay, fine. But it's not my fault if you pop up on the other side split into a dozen pieces like ice cubes popped out of a tray."

"I'm not worried," Sirene says.

"So where am I going?"

"I doubt you even have to think about it." She places her hand on my shoulder. "Where do you feel drawn?"

I regard her with suspicion. "What do you mean?"

She just stares at me as if urging me to answer my own question.

And then—

Distantly, somewhere far, far beyond this office building, there's a subtle tug. The feeling I get reminds me of playing hide and seek as a kid, like I need to get home free, and put my hand on the bark of the oak designated as home.

There's a pop, a rushing in my ears.

The stairwell is gone and replaced immediately with four stone walls.

When I speak, my voice echoes. "Where are we?"

Weak light shines through a domed glass ceiling. There are more windows along the perimeter, most of them coated in grime and overwhelmed by roots and cobwebs.

It reminds me of the mausoleum where we brought Chaos over.

But this isn't the same place. This one is bigger, more ornate, and at the head of the room above the stone doorway is a new symbol.

The bright sun.

"This is another *porta limina*," Sirene says. "Portal of Worship."

"For who?"

But I already know before she tells me.

"The Bright Goddess."

Divine Mother, Reignyabit, Reign.

I'm going to be sick.

I bend over in the corner and retch, but nothing comes up. I brace myself on the wall, choking on air as my stomach tries to revolt and comes up empty.

Sirene's hand settles between my shoulder blades, then moves my hair aside.

Bile comes up, burning my throat, burning in the back of my nose.

I keep gagging.

This isn't real.

It can't be fucking real.

When the retching stops and I'm able to take a deep breath, Sirene tears a strip of cloth from her shirt and hands it to me to wipe my mouth.

If the power, the names, the portal of worship wasn't proof enough, this wet length of cloth is.

Sirene isn't the type of woman to destroy her clothes for a bit of common spit.

Somehow, it's that that makes me break.

"I can't do this." I love him, is what I don't say.

And he'll never forgive me for this.

He's terrified of losing his power and his throne.

I can't have power majority.

My nose burns again, but this time with unshed tears.

"Yes, you can," Sirene says.

"Then I don't want to."

"You were born for this."

"Because of you." I grit my teeth. "*You* did this."

"Do you want to hear it?"

I ball the strip of fabric in my hand. "Hear what?"

"The story of Reignyabit and why I betrayed a king to give birth to a goddess."

CHAPTER
FOURTEEN

I want to go home but where is home now? Where the hell do I belong?

All of me has been carved out and filled with something new that I don't recognize.

I find a stone bench and drop onto it. Sirene goes to the closed portal and admires it, her back to me. "Everything I've told you is still true. Wrath did give me these scars." She runs her fingers gently over the puckered skin as if the scar still hurts. "Chaos did start WWII, but Wrath was just as complicit. He didn't try to stop Chaos and he should have. They had both grown too powerful, too greedy for their own good."

She steps away from the portal wall. "When there's war, Oracle activity intensifies. Are you familiar with them? The Oracles?"

I nod. "I met one with Ciri when she first came to the castle."

"What did it tell you?"

I sit forward, prop my elbows on my knees. "Something about Chaos. Umm... 'through Chaos, there is order. Through order, there is peace. Through you, there is redemption. You are the only way. So you must do as you must and do it quickly.'"

Sirene rolls her eyes. "Ciri liked to speak in riddles, but the Oracles are another level." She comes over to me. "The death and carnage of WWII brought out the Oracles in droves. And when there's increased Oracle activity, inevitably there are whispers of the future.

"I kept hearing about Reignyabit. I only had a vague understanding of her. For being the mother of all, she was pretty much wiped from our books and oral histories. Even in Alius, men take credit for everything, even the birth of the world."

She paces away, her hands on her hips. "Those who would *listen* started to *believe* and places like this were built to worship her in the hopes that she would come to end the suffering. When people suffer, they always prefer the feminine hand, the gentle goddess."

Sirene laughs and the sound bubbles around us in an echo. "Of course, Reignyabit was never gentle and of course she didn't come. Gods and Goddesses don't just pop up out of thin air. That's not how it works. Never has, never will. But—"

"You knew that the Demon King supposedly possessed the power handed down from the Dark God."

She turns to meet my gaze. "Exactly. I had never met a goddess, but I had lived my entire life surrounded by *power*. Power that could do incredible things."

I rise to my feet.

"I knew it would be impossible for me to take any of the triad from the Demon King," she says, "but he and Chaos were at odds."

"Why?"

"Do you remember the story I told you? Of the village Wrath destroyed when he was trying to put down a coup to overthrow him?"

122

I nod.

"There was a girl there...a vampire. She was a daughter of the family that wanted to overthrow Wrath. Chaos was in love with her. Truth be told, she was using him, but his love was real."

The revelation hits me like a stone to the face.

The pain of the loss, even though it isn't mine, is acute.

I know what it is to love something. But I can't imagine what it is to lose it.

It must feel like your heart is being torn out of your chest.

I don't want to feel sorry for Chaos, but it's impossible not to.

"So when you approached Chaos with the idea of taking the *animus* from Wrath—"

"He was more than willing to do it."

"What did you tell him though?" I trail her as she circles the room. "Obviously, you didn't tell him you planned to birth a goddess."

She snorts. "Obviously. He did try to keep it at first, but he ran into the same issue he had with the *oculus*. There's a reason Wrath was chosen to be king. Chaos was never strong enough. But hubris is always the best way to make a man bend to your will. I told him that I'd hold the *animus* in a safe place until it was his time to rule. That surely it was his destiny. He was happy to believe me."

At the portal, she stops again, crosses her arms over her chest. "I've always believed that whatever I want done, I can do. I don't doubt myself." She looks over at me. "But you"—she gestures at me with a wave of her hand—"what you've become... to be honest with you, Rain, I doubted this was even possible and yet here you are."

Here I am.

The supposed reincarnation of an ancient goddess.

I keep waiting for someone to pull a prank card and laugh at me for even believing a grain of it as truth.

But it never comes.

Sirene doesn't laugh. She levels me with an intense gaze and it's her belief in me, in what I am, that scares me the most.

"What do you want me to do?" I ask. "What do you think I *can* do?"

She looks me right in the eyes and says, "You'll take the last of the Demon King's power and you will reign."

FIFTEEN

I'M NOT SURPRISED BY HER PLAN, BUT I AM GOING TO IGNORE IT.

"I'm not going to overthrow the Demon King and steal a throne to another world. That wasn't one of my life goals."

Sirene stands in front of the stone portal. "The Demon King has reigned long enough. His entire ancestral line, all of them men, ruling with brutality and greed. You have the opportunity to stop him."

I scoff. "I will admit that using the whole feminine power thing is pretty potent on me. You know my mom."

She gives me a genuine smile. "Why do you think I picked your mother as a vessel? Sunny Low is a badass bitch."

I laugh. "Yeah, she is. But...this is more complex than the patriarchy."

She nods. "You're more than a symbolism of feminine power."

"Symbolism." I snort. "I'm no symbol."

"You will be."

"I can't be your Joan of Arc, Sirene."

"I don't want a saint, Rain. I want a fucking god."

"Well, you're not getting that either." I turn to the nearest wall and start running my hands through the tangle of vines, looking for a door. "Now how do I get out of this place?'

"Rain."

I ignore her and keep searching.

"Rain."

"What?"

"Your back—it's glowing."

"What?!" I spin around, but of course I can't see my back.

"Here." Sirene goes to the nearest window and with nothing more than a flick of her wrist, the vines disintegrate, revealing the glass. There's just enough of a reflection that I can see between my shoulder blades where a distinct bright glow is emanating from my skin.

I yank the shirt off to get a better look.

"It's my birthmark." The same one that Wrath freaked out about when I was caught naked and soaking wet. "Why is it doing that?"

"I don't know," Sirene admits.

"How do I stop it?"

Her eyes are wide.

"Sirene."

"I don't know. This is new territory for me."

"Fucking hell. How do I—"

Like a bell tolling, I sense Wrath searching for me, drawing nearer.

My first thought is—thank god he's all right.

My second thought is—oh shit.

"What is it?" Sirene asks. "Is it the mark? Are you okay?"

"No. I mean...yes. It's Wrath. He's coming for me."

Her eyes narrow. "Of course he is."

"You should go."

"What do you plan to do?"

"I don't know. How the fuck do I get out of here?"

"You can literally transport yourself anywhere in the world."

I grumble. "I'm still learning how to drive, all right?"

The connection between Wrath and me intensifies, thrums brighter. He's close.

"You need to go," I tell Sirene.

"Fine. But if you need me—"

"I'm sure I can find you."

She waves her hand in the air, eyes glowing green. The vines pull away to reveal a door to a forest beyond. I follow her out.

Night has fallen wherever we are and the air is cool. It's mostly hardwood trees with a few tall, skinny pines. I marvel all over again at being able to hear things I should not hear. Like the rasp of pine needles, an animal digging beneath my feet, the skittering of claws on tree bark somewhere far away.

I want to deny that any of this is real, but how can I when literally everything has changed?

"Good luck, Rain," Sirene says.

I get the distinct impression she means *Reign* this time and it makes me shiver.

She starts off and disappears through a grove of pines.

My belly warms as Wrath draws nearer. I get a sense of panic followed by relief through our connection. He knows I'm all right—he was worried I wasn't.

My heart drums in my ears.

He's going to be pissed.

What happens after this?

I have two-thirds of the Demon King's power. He's not going to handle that well.

When he appears several yards away still shrouded in darkness, I can see all of the hard lines of his body, the slant of his cheekbones, the sharp cut of his jaw.

"Hi," I say, trying not to be awkward as fuck.

127

"You're all right," he says. The connection thrums with relief.

"I am. And you?"

"Alive."

"Good."

He comes closer and finds a pocket of moonlight. "Who took you?"

"It's a super long story and—"

"Rain." His expression sharpens, his voice rumbles. "Who took you?"

"It was MAW at first, but they were working for Chaos."

His jaw flexes.

"But I'm okay now."

"But something is different." It's not a question.

I swallow loudly and of course, the Demon King notices. His eyes narrow, gray flecks flaring red in the night as he reads me as easily as an open book.

"You have the *oculus*."

A coyote howls in the distance.

"Not on purpose."

The red in his eyes intensifies.

"Chaos couldn't hold on to it."

The monster swims to the surface.

"I didn't ask for it."

"And yet you have it just the same. Tell me this wasn't your plan all along."

"Of course it wasn't! They tricked me into taking it."

He cants his head, his body going rigid with distrust. "Tricked you into taking one of the most powerful objects in the world?"

"I—yes. I swear it. This was not my plan. I had no plan!"

"Poor, innocent Rain, gifted with power she never wanted."

"Hey." I jab my finger into his chest. "That's not fair. I had a life before all of this, you know."

He stalks away, forcing me to chase after him.

"Wait. Will you please stop?"

He whirls around, his eyes glowing bright crimson now. The monster lurks just below the surface.

"Funny," the Demon King says, "I had a life before you too."

"Okay, asshole, but how was that going for you? The whole reason we're in this mess is because you burned down that village with the *animus* and killed that woman Chaos loved."

He comes to a halt, body rigid.

"So it's true?" I suddenly feel sick.

He turns his head, the sharp line of his jaw standing out in stark relief against the darkness beyond him. "It was a coup. What else was I to do?"

"He loved her."

"A king can't bend for love."

I stagger back as if he's slapped me.

He warned me though, didn't he? He told me he couldn't love me the way I deserved. I thought we could figure out a way to love each other the best ways we knew how. I thought maybe we could be equals, that we could do this together.

But as usual, I'm alone in this. I've always been alone. I've always done everything myself.

"Do you wish to steal my throne, *dieva*?"

I swallow again, take in a deep breath. "Is that all you're worried about?"

Slowly, he turns to me, all of the light gone from his eyes. "Answer me."

Tears blur in my vision. Through the connection, I can almost taste his fear and his undying devotion to doing what he must. Love doesn't factor into it at all. And neither does trust.

"You are terrified of being powerless," I say, "so you do terrible things to prove you aren't. What will you do to me?"

"Answer the fucking question."

In this moment, the only thing I want to do is hurt him.

I don't care how I do it.

I don't care what the consequences are.

I just want him to feel this aching pain, the sharp cut of heartbreak.

Teeth clenched, tears burning in my eyes, I say, "And what if I did?"

The connection between us thrums immediately with rage as the monster comes out and he darts across the clearing, taking me by the throat. He runs me back, slams me into a tree and the old me braces for the impact, waits for the ache of lost oxygen and the overwhelming feeling of being powerless.

But it doesn't come.

There is no pain.

The impact barely registers at all even though the tree shakes and the leaves tremble from the impact.

The only thing I feel is the tug of more power.

The last bit of the triad.

The *dominus*. The only thing the Demon King still possesses.

And it's calling to me.

In this moment, there is one thought running through my mind: *take it.*

If you want it, take it.

I can render him completely powerless and make his worst fears come true.

He doesn't love me. He can't possibly love me.

The only thing he cares about is power.

He's no better than the Dark Father God, destroying what he must to have what he wants.

Wrath's eyes go wide.

His demon mark flares beneath his shirt.

His grip on me tightens. "*Dieva.*" My name is a growl in the base of his throat, filled with pain and surprise.

A knot untangles, a bow comes undone.

Heat flares beneath Wrath's grip, but it's not coming from him, it's coming from me.

The connection vibrates.

"*Rain.*"

He strains against me, fingers pressing hard on my throat as he tries to pull away. But he can't. He can't break the contact because I control it.

"*Dieva!*"

Power flares through me, igniting my insides, beating at my core.

I'm overcome with a sense of rightness that fills my veins, hollows out my bones.

Fire crackles along my skin. Golden light blooms in the clearing.

And as the glow of Wrath's demon mark fades, a new mark appears on my chest, ancient ink sinking beneath layers of skin.

I know the second the *dominus* comes to me. It's one final piece clicking into place.

I don't even have to take the stone from him. I don't need a vessel to claim it.

My belly soars at the victory of it.

Wrath backpedals, skin pale, eyes dull gray. He's breathing heavily, dark brow sunk in a V.

I took the last of his power.

I took it with barely any effort at all.

And worse, the connection between us is gone, leaving that steady thrum between us silent and broken. I immediately feel hollow without it and left out in the cold.

But maybe this was our destiny all along.

Maybe we were never meant to love and be loved.

He warned me and I didn't listen.

The Demon King can't love.

But I wanted him to. I wanted us to be different than we are.

"I didn't want your throne," I tell him. "I wanted you to trust me."

"How could I?" he counters. "When you betrayed me around every turn."

I don't know what to do with myself or where to go but I know I can't stay here.

I turn around to leave, feeling both flush with power and overwhelmed with heartbreak.

"*Dieva*."

I look at him over my shoulder.

"It takes more than power to rule."

I know what he's left unsaid—do I have what it takes?

Hell no, I don't.

But I'm caught in the hurricane now, battling forces beyond my control.

I'm desperate to anchor myself to something and the first person that pops into my head is Gus.

I need Gus.

I need my best friend.

This time, I don't even have to think about it.

My completed triad of power—the *animus*, the *oculus*, the *dominus*—pulls me away, leaving the Demon King alone with nothing.

CHAPTER
SIXTEEN

I DON'T KNOW WHERE I'M GOING WHEN I THINK OF GUS. ONLY THAT I want to be by his side.

Somehow the power knows where to find him and I pop up in his kitchen in his condo in Norton Harbor.

Adam is there with him.

"Holy shit," Gus says and drops the bottle of ketchup in his hand. The top pops open and red sauce squirts on the white cabinets and splatters on the floor.

Adam has pulled a gun in two seconds flat and has the barrel pointed at me.

I hold up my hands. "I come unarmed."

Sort of.

Does an ancient triad of divine power count?

Fuck if that doesn't sound like the craziest shit ever.

"Rain," Gus says and then he's rushing me, wrapping me in the wide span of his arms. I take in a deep breath, grateful to smell his familiar smell. Tea and baked goods and beneath that, the scent of his soap, his shaving cream, and a hint of Adam.

When Gus lets me go, I turn to his boyfriend. Stoic, all-business Adam doesn't hesitate to envelop me. And for some reason, it's Adam's comfort and compassion that makes me start bawling.

And as my body shakes and I lose control of the tears, Gus comes up behind me, sandwiching me between them.

"It's okay," Gus says.

Adam hugs me, steady and solid. "We got you, Rain."

I don't know how long I break down in their arms, but they let me, holding me close in their warmth and their love.

I wanted to think that I could handle this alone, always alone, but now I realize how much bullshit that is.

I need them.

I need someone who knew me before all of this happened.

Before I became—

I'm not going to think it. I'm not going to say the word.

Because there is no way in hell I'm a reincarnated goddess.

No. Way. In. Hell.

Adam has a tissue ready for me when we pull apart and I make a mess of it, drying my eyes and blowing my nose.

"Sit," Gus says and pulls out one of the barstools at the L-shaped counter. The same place we spent many nights getting drunk and bullshitting about anything and everything.

God, I miss that.

"Here." Adam pours me a glass of wine. Gus fills me a plate with homemade sweet potato fries and waffles, then drenches the pile of food in local maple syrup. "Eat," Gus says.

"I'm not sure I have much of an appetite," I tell him and then literally three minutes later the plate is empty. "Ummm... ha...okay, maybe I was hungry. What else do you have?"

"Dessert?" Gus lifts a brow. "I have several leftover pastries from Olga's from the tea shop. If you want—"

"Yes. Gimme." I waggle my fingers at him.

Once it's in my hand, I devour two of the treats. Usually by now I'd be stuffed and near comatose. But I feel like I haven't eaten a thing.

"Are you okay?" Gus finally asks.

Adam pours me another glass of wine. The alcohol hasn't even touched me.

"I don't know."

I feel so...different.

"Talk to us." Gus sets his wine glass down. The cross earring that dangles from his ear swings back and forth as he folds his arms on the counter and hunches toward me. "You know you can tell us anything. We're here for you."

I wave him away. "While I appreciate that, what I really need is for us to *not* talk about me. Give me something normal. What about you guys? What's going on with you?"

They share a look and a clever little smile comes to Gus's mouth.

"What?"

"You want to tell her or should I?" Gus asks Adam.

"The honor is yours." Adam leans into the corner of the L-shaped counter and props the heels of his hands on the edge. The sleeves of his t-shirt rise on the dip of his biceps, revealing some of his ink.

"Tell me what?"

The smile on Gus's face widens and his heart starts beating faster. I can hear it as plainly as if I had my ear to his chest. In fact, not only can I hear it beating, I can smell his excitement, this tangy, sharpness on the air.

And then, faintly, almost like a whisper, I hear him think —*married*.

"You're engaged?" I blurt.

Both he and Adam look at me wide-eyed.

Oh, fuck.

Which part of the Demon King's power can read and manipulate minds?

I don't remember, but I have it now and now I can...fuck.

"How did you know?" Gus frowns at me. "Way to steal my thunder."

"This...you...I'm sorry." I stumble away from the barstool.

Worried about her.

She's different.

Now I can hear Adam and Gus. Both of their voices in my head, but none of the words spoken aloud.

No no no.

"Rain?"

Swallowing, raking my teeth over my bottom lip, I focus on getting my shit together.

I can't let on what's happening. Gus will never feel comfortable around me. Maybe there's a way to control it. Maybe I should ask—

I almost thought to ask Wrath for pointers on how to shut it off. I'm sure he'll be all too happy to help.

Yeah, right.

I'm on my own with this one.

I swallow, smile as genuinely as I possibly can and clap my hands together. "This is such great news! Congratulations!" I give them both hugs and feel a little hollow inside as I do.

This should be the happiest news I've heard in a long time. My best friend is getting married!

And I'm fucking breaking inside because the Demon King thinks I betrayed him—again—and I stole his power. All of it.

All of it is mine and I don't know what the fuck I'm supposed to do with it.

I can't rule a world.

I don't want a throne.

My entire life, I've been alone, depending mostly on myself.

But the thought of doing this without Wrath leaves me hollow inside.

And hearing my best friend is getting married to someone he loves makes me burn with envy.

I want that.

I didn't know I did until—

Adam's phone chimes. He checks the screen and silences the ring. "I gotta take this." He gives Gus a squeeze on the shoulder and disappears into the other room, shutting the door behind him.

Gus must catch me watching his boyfriend, because he adds, "Lots has been going on in the military lately. As I'm sure you can imagine."

I nod, blink, and turn back to him. "Do you know what their plans are? For Wrath?"

I hate to get nosy and use my best friend for inside info, but this is one instance I'm willing to throw down all my moral codes.

"I know they're planning something with Chaos at the helm and that he's been making them promises they're salivating over."

"What kind of promises?"

Gus tilts his head, his mouth turning down. "What do old white men in power do best?"

They invade. Conquer. Enslave. Steal.

"They can't seriously be thinking of going to Alius, can they?"

Gus straightens, scratches at the back of his head. "You know I only hear the barest of details. It's all highly classified. Blah blah blah." He rolls his eyes. "But—and I didn't hear this from Adam, just to be clear. I'm not breaking his trust. I got it from Harper."

"Harper?"

Gus nods. "She overheard her dad and General Briggs talking about it. Chaos has promised to help the military take out Wrath so that Chaos can assume the throne. But in exchange, he's asked to take several troops with him to his world. Apparently, they don't have guns there, so soldiers with big weapons might help him keep control of the world.

"But you think they seriously mean to just hand him a throne?"

"Hell no. Long term game plan is to kill Chaos too."

I lean in. "Do you know that for a fact?"

"That's what Harper said.

"How long ago was that?"

Gus shrugs. "A few days, I think?"

That was before Chaos lost the *oculus*, before I was the one who took on the triad.

I'm not sure if this is a good or bad thing. They'll still want to handle Wrath. They won't leave that threat unchecked, regardless of how much power he still has.

But when they find out I technically have the Demon King's power...that I'm the way to the throne...

Did Sirene think this one through? Did Chaos, for that matter?

I can hear Gus's thoughts again, like a quiet breeze whistling through a crack in the wall.

Worried. So worried. Different.

I need to get out of here. The room is starting to feel stuffy and suffocating. I need...

"Want to go up to the rooftop?"

Gus looks over his shoulder at the closed bedroom door. "He'll probably be a while. Why not?"

"I'm bringing a new bottle of wine."

"I'll grab the corkscrew and a blanket."

Just a few minutes later, we're making our way down the hallway and to the stairwell and up to the rooftop access.

The wind cuts in across the roof, tossing my hair in my face. I spin into it and somehow smell everything.

Literally everything.

It's like watching a movie for the first time in technicolor.

Sensing my distress as a chill, Gus drapes the blanket over my shoulders and tugs it tightly to my chest.

"Thanks," I say.

Using the corkscrew, he pops out the cork from the wine and drinks straight from the bottle. Leading me to the north side of the building where the harbor glitters with moonlight three blocks away, we climb up on the emergency stairwell and sit on the first landing.

We've spent so many nights here that they all blur together, but it's as familiar as a bed.

"Tell me about the Demon King," he says. "What happened?"

I sigh heavily. "It's...complicated."

"I figured as much."

He takes another swig off the bottle and hands it to me. Down on the quiet street, a car passes playing loud pop music. The people inside sing along laughing.

"I bound myself to him," I tell Gus and he somehow takes this news with barely any reaction. "And then I found out from Sirene—"

"The witch."

"Yup. I found out that she thinks I'm a reincarnated goddess from Alius." I snort, laugh, take another drink. "As if I didn't have enough problems on my plate."

Gus rolls his eyes. "I hear you, babes. To find out you're a reborn goddess? I mean, come on. Who even has time for that?"

I laugh. He smiles.

"I mean it, though. Like...she really thinks I'm a goddess. Or something."

He looks over at me, the moonlight skimming his face, streaking his curls in pale, silver light. "I know. I *hear* you. I always do."

"But aren't you shocked?"

"I'm not sure anything could shock me at this point."

The fact that he's not freaking out, that he's taking the news calmly, rationally, makes me want to sob in his arms. Gus makes me feel sane.

"I miss you every waking minute we're apart," I tell him.

"I miss you too."

Stealing the bottle back, he takes a long pull and then winds his arm around my shoulders, drawing me into his side while he sticks the bottle between his knees.

Gus feels like home too. Familiar and safe.

"You know, I'm not surprised that you're a primordial being."

"Stop! I am not."

He makes a *pfffttt* sound. "Should we return to Ben Hightower?"

"Me punching Ben Hightower in his stupid nose has nothing to do with being a reincarnated goddess."

"I beg to differ."

I meet his gaze and then we both burst out laughing.

"You ever wonder what stupid Ben Hightower is doing?" I ask and wiggle my fingers for the bottle.

"Actually, yes. I am a glutton for punishment, remember? I look him up from time to time. You'll never guess what I saw on his feed last time I stalked him."

"Oh, do tell!"

He smiles devilishly. "He's gay. Like legit has a boyfriend. Damn fine too if I'm being honest."

"What?" My voice echoes down the street and a dog barks in an apartment across the intersection.

"Shhh!" Gus puts his finger over his mouth even though we're both laughing uncontrollably now.

"That fucking asshole called you a fairy. That's the whole reason I punched him."

Gus shrugs. "I guess he was projecting."

"I guess so."

The dog keeps barking. Our bottle of wine gets closer to the bottom.

"I'm really happy for you and Adam."

Gus squeezes my shoulder. "Thank you. You'll be my best man, right?"

"Absolutely. It would be my greatest honor. Did you set a date yet?"

"No. We figured we better wait until all of *this* settles down." He gestures vaguely with his free hand and even though he doesn't say it, I know he means me. Me and the Demon King.

I take another drink, leaving one last gulp in the bottom for Gus. His cheeks have turned rosy and he's starting to slur.

I still feel nothing.

In fact, the longer I have this power running through my veins, the better I feel. The more *other* I feel.

"Gus," I say, my gaze trained on the harbor in the distance where a moored sailboat bobs with the waves.

"Yeah?"

"How do you know it's love?"

He drains the last of the bottle and sets it on the roof behind us. "Well..." He rubs his hands together like he's cold, so I open the blanket and yank him into it. We huddle together as the night grows colder.

He thinks on his answer for a minute, his attention fixed on the flagpole on the roof across from us. The flag snaps in the wind and Gus tightens the blanket around us.

"It's like this," he says, gesturing to the blanket. "It's that feeling you get when you've had a shitty day and you come home, you strip out of your clothes and you make a hot drink or a stiff one and you curl up in the blanket watching *Great British Bake Off* and suddenly everything feels fuzzy and warm."

He smiles to himself, running his tongue over his bottom lip. "I have that feeling every time Adam wraps his arms around me. Being with him is like a deep breath. Both the inhale and the exhale."

I immediately flash back to being in Wrath's bed, to him taking me in his arms when he thought I was asleep.

Him breathing deeply, then sighing against my neck.

Like a deep breath.

My chest tightens.

My chin wobbles.

"Rain?"

"I have to go."

"What? Where?"

I throw the blanket back and climb down from the stair landing.

"Rain!"

"I have to go to him."

"Who?"

Gus catches up to me and grabs me by the hand, pulling me to a stop. "You're crying. Why are you crying?"

"Gus."

"Talk to me, babes."

"I think I love him."

"The Demon King?"

I nod. "I know it sounds crazy. It *is* crazy."

"It's not crazy."

I pull to a stop. "It's not?"

"I mean...okay, it's a little out of this world. Maybe literally. But you can't help what the heart wants."

"Spoken like a true greeting card."

"Adam would be proud."

"I've yet to see his romantic side. Can we force him to write his own vows and say them in front of everyone at your wedding?"

"I'll bribe him." Gus winks at me. "I am persuasive."

"I have to go," I say again.

"Okay. But promise me you'll let me know you're all right."

"I promise."

He pulls me into one last hug and kisses my temple. "Go get the demon."

I laugh. "He might try to murder me, but what's love without murder?"

"This doesn't sound healthy."

"I'm a goddess, apparently. I'm sure I can survive."

I step back and think of Wrath. I know in an instant where he is and my newfound power pulls me away without any effort at all.

SEVENTEEN

I REAPPEAR AT THE STABLES AT THE CASTLE, WHICH INSTANTLY PUTS ME on guard.

The castle is no longer a safe location and I can smell the burning wreckage of it across the property.

The stables are mostly dark, but with my new power, I can see every grain in the wood in the walls, every divot in the stone floor. The muskiness of horses and the earthiness of hay fills the air.

But beneath that is fear, panic, dread, and Chaos.

I spot the brothers at the end of the stable aisle.

Out of sight, I sense several men and women hidden in the stalls and beyond.

I know for a fact one of them is Ryder.

Oh, how I yearn to tear that man's spine through his nostrils.

"I told you she'd come," Chaos says.

A lantern flickers on, shooting soft golden light across the aisle.

Wrath is at the end with Sirene beside him, Chaos and his stolen *norrow* lined up in front. Even though he lost the oculus, he apparently still holds some sway over them. But for how long?

And that begs the question—can I control the *norrow*?

There is a deep-seated awareness of them that runs along my skin like a spider in the darkness. I've never felt it quite like that before.

To my left, Ryder and several of his men stand equidistance apart like sentinels at a gate, their massive guns in hand, fingers poised dangerously close to the triggers.

"What is this?" I ask.

"*Dieva*," Wrath says with a labored intake of breath. There's blood on the air, *his* blood. Somehow the mighty Demon King has been cut and I'm left untouched.

I sensed our connection dying when I took the last of the triad, but it still surprises me that I am not connected to this wound, that I can't share in his pain.

I did this to him.

I left him vulnerable.

I never should have run from him.

"You did what none of us have been able to do," Chaos says. "You rendered the Demon King nearly powerless."

I step closer. "I don't want his throne. I've never even been to your world."

Chaos waves my fears away. "It's a lot like yours. Just with more demons and vampires and witches."

"Somehow I doubt that. What do you want from me, Chaos?"

"You hold all of the power now." He steps forward and the *norrow* follow him. "I can't take it from you and I don't want to."

"What you mean to say is, you can't."

He laughs, nods and then pushes his glasses back on the bridge of his nose with a press of his index finger. "I can help you, Rain. You have the power, I have the knowledge and the clout. Half of Alius has wanted Wrath gone for a very long time. They'll be happy to follow someone else, especially someone as pretty as you."

Wrath growls. Sirene waves her hand and magic glitters on the air. She's holding him hostage somehow.

"What you want is a puppet," I guess and though I think he's trying very hard to shield himself from me, I still hear his thoughts.

Tell her what she wants to hear.

"We will be equals."

It's like he's been eavesdropping on me and Wrath this entire time.

That's what I always wanted.

I fold my arms over my chest. "You do know that the president and the general plan to get rid of you too, right?"

He flinches. He didn't know.

"They're plotting a coup behind your back. Once Wrath is gone, you'll be next." I nod at Ryder. "I bet he knows the plan."

Ryder rocks his shoulders back. "She's lying."

But his thoughts say otherwise—*fucking bitch is about to blow this thing. Keep it calm. Can wait to gut her and fuck her and show her how powerless she is.*

Wrath taught me how not to let the rage take hold, but even he must know that sometimes it's the only thing.

If Ryder thinks of me that way, I can only imagine what he's done to other women who don't have a Demon King to save them and an ancient power running through their veins.

Does he really think he can rape me?

Sometimes rage is warranted.

I disappear and slip into the sub-dimension. It's nothing more than a blink, a slight pressure, and I've left one place and reappeared in another. Right in front of Ryder. He has a foot on me and easily a hundred pounds of weight, most of it muscle.

He flinches, recovers, then sneers down at me.

"Did no one teach you how to respect women?"

He runs his tongue along the inside of his bottom lip. "I respect those who've earned it."

"You shouldn't have to earn the right to be treated like a human being."

"Rain," Sirene says and starts toward me.

But it's too late.

I've had enough of Ryder and the desire to tear his limbs from his body is overriding anything else.

How dare he.

How fucking dare he.

When my eyes glow, the golden light is reflected in Ryder's gaze. He clenches his teeth and moves his finger to the trigger.

"Rain, wait!" Sirene darts forward.

Chaos curses and orders the *norrow* to stop me.

Flames ignite in my hand and lick up my arms.

Not afraid of this demon cunt, Ryder thinks as his soldiers grow antsy around us, sensing the impending violence.

I reach out with my hand and Ryder whips his gun forward, pointing the barrel at my gut.

He pulls the trigger and nothing happens.

All of the smug bravado slips from his stupid fucking face.

"Now what, asshole?" I say, but I don't give him the chance to answer.

I place my hand on his forearm and his skin chars and starts flaking away into ash.

His mouth opens in an O but no sound comes out as the flames eat away at his body like dry tinder in a wildfire.

One minute Ryder is standing in front of me and the next he's disintegrating into ash.

His soldiers take formation around me. "Kill the bitch," one of them says, and bullets start flying.

"Rain!" Wrath shouts. There's the telltale sound of cloth snapping in the wind and then Wrath is behind me, wrapping his arms around me, shielding me as bullets pummel him.

His body jerks taking the hits and I slam into a horse stall as his weight comes down on me.

Blood permeates the air.

"Stop!" Sirene yells. "Fucking stop shooting!" There's a sharp crackle, grown men groaning and then slamming against the opposite stall.

"Wrath?" He's dead weight on top of me. "Wrath!" I shimmy out from beneath him and push him over so I can see his face and—

There's so much blood. Too much.

The Demon King isn't supposed to bleed so easily.

Fuck. Fuck. This isn't happening.

I have to do something.

Ryder's men climb to their feet, guns back in hand.

"Wrath!" I shake him but he doesn't respond, his eyes closed, his mouth slack. Is his heart still beating? I don't have time to check him.

The big guy at the front sees the Demon King down and triumph flickers in his eyes.

I'm not letting them take him.

I'm not going to let him die.

Planting my butt on the stone floor, I hook my arms beneath Wrath's and pull him back.

Please, divine power, don't fail me now.

Pressure builds around me as heat ignites in my chest.

In a blink, we're gone.

EIGHTEEN

LIKE MOST OF MY PRIMORDIAL TRAVEL, I DON'T THINK ABOUT WHERE TO go, but my instincts carry me anyway.

And when we reappear with a crash in my former biological father's studio, I'm shocked and relieved to see my mom there.

"Mom?"

"Rain? What the—is that the Demon King? Rainy baby! Why is he...he's bleeding everywhere."

Jeffrey rushes over. He's still wearing his work apron and flecks of marble cover the front. "What happened?"

I try to explain but I'm sobbing and I can't catch my breath.

He's going to die.

I can't lose him.

I can't do this without him.

"I need help," I manage to choke out.

Jeffrey cleans off the nearest table with a quick swipe of his arm. Tools, chunks of marble, and several bottles of solvent crash to the floor.

Mom and Jeffrey are all business. "Get his feet," Jeffrey says. "I'll get under his arms."

Together, all three of us carry Wrath from the floor and hoist him up on the table.

He's so incredibly pale. Blood is smudged across his face, painting his lips in streaks of crimson.

Jeffrey tears off Wrath's shirt to assess the wounds. "Sunny," he says, "grab my tool bag over there. It's on the bench."

Mom hurries over and grabs what's needed. She pulls out a pair of hemostats and hands them off. "Rain," Jeffrey says, "we'll need some wet rags and a bucket of water. Do you think he needs sterile tools? Isn't he invincible?"

"He was...before I took his power."

"You *what*?" Mom's eyes go round.

"I didn't mean to."

"There's a small kitchenette through that door," Jeffrey says, focusing on the problem at hand. I'm glad someone else can think straight. "Start boiling water. Can you do that?"

I gulp, catch on a sob.

He's not moving. His face is so still. I am gutted. Hollow.

"Rain?"

I blink back to Jeffrey. "Yes," I say. "I can do it."

"Go. Hurry."

I grope around for a light switch in the side room before I realize I can see everything in the dark. I grab a pot from the sink and fill it with water, fidgeting while I wait for the fucking thing to fill up.

Faster, goddammit.

Once the pot is full, I set it on the stove and light the burner and then return to Wrath. Jeffrey is currently digging out bullets from over two dozen bullet holes, Mom assisting him.

"Is he..." I trail off, unable to ask the question out loud.

"His heart is still beating," Jeffrey says as he gingerly removes a bullet and drops it into a bloody Mason jar.

Hope steals my breath.

Jeffrey pulls out two more bullets.

"I have his power. I can probably heal him." I rush over to the table. "Maybe I should just—"

Jeffrey puts his arm out. "No. Not yet. The bullets need to come out first before he can be healed, magic or no magic."

"How's that water, baby?" Mom asks.

I return to the kitchen to find the surface flat. "Fucking hell." This needs to go faster.

I call on my power and then stick my hand into the pot. Immediately the water is boiling hot.

Okay. I can do this. I can be useful.

I dunk several cloths I find in a cupboard into the water and pace the tiny kitchen. How long does it take to sterilize cloth? I don't even know.

When I think enough time has passed, I carry the pot out into the main room. The Mason jar is filling up with bullets and the table is drenched in the Demon King's blood.

I don't feel his pain anymore but I'm gutted just the same.

"We need to get him on his stomach," Jeffrey says. "The rest of the bullets are in his back."

It takes us some effort, but we manage to turn him around. There are nine more wounds dotting his skin from his shoulders down to the small of his back and as Jeffrey pulls out the bullets, I mop up the mess, being gentle with the swipe of the cloth.

By the time Jeffrey is done, the sun is rising in the windows of his studio and Wrath is still unconscious.

"I have a small bed in the back room." Jeffrey nods at a closed door beyond his latest marble sculpture. "We should move him there."

It takes us another ten minutes to shuffle Wrath across the studio, his massive body suspended between all three of us. Mom grunts beside me. Jeffrey does his best with Wrath's legs.

When we set him on the bed, the wooden frame lets out a loud complaint.

"Can you heal him, baby?" Mom asks. She hovers behind me, her arms crossed over her chest. There's blood on her hands.

"Maybe. I think so."

"We'll give you a minute," she says and Jeffrey follows her out.

I go to the bedside. There's a large window above the bed that looks out over the field behind Jeffrey's house. The sunlight paints the tall grass in saturated gold.

And on the bed, the Demon King is so fucking pale, it terrifies me.

Why did he step in front of me? What the fuck was he thinking? I have the triad. I would have been fine—I think.

It doesn't make any sense.

I kneel on the floor and take his hand in mine. Veins bulge beneath the skin, twining around his knuckles. I run my fingertip over one, trace it across his wrist and up his arm.

He doesn't even flinch.

"Don't do this to me," I whisper. "I've always thought I was strong enough to shoulder things alone. I've always just taken care of myself, depended on no one but myself. But now I realize...I was just terrified of loving something so much that losing it would break me."

Tears blur my vision and I sniff them back. "And look, I think that's turning out to be true. If you were awake right now, you'd be rolling your eyes at me and saying something in that cocky, smarmy voice of yours, '*Did you learn your lesson, dieva?*' Well, yes. Okay. I learned my fucking lesson. I can't do this alone." I thread my fingers with his and squeeze. "I need you to wake up."

I stare at his face so hard, my eyes burn.

"Wrath."

Nothing.

"Wrath!"

My power rushes to the surface filling the room with bright light. Maybe if I push it toward him—

The acrid scent of burning flesh permeates the air.

"Fuck!" I drop Wrath's hand as his skin blisters and peels back leaving raw, festering wounds. "Fuck!"

The rage, the despair overwhelms me, engulfs me.

I'm like a bomb about to explode.

I can't think straight. My vision pulses white on the edges.

I did this.

I didn't want this.

My hands tremble and burn with fire. Heat blooms in the room.

"Rain!" Mom comes into the doorway and then throws up her arm as the heat ribbons around her.

I have to get out of here.

I want to destroy something.

I let the power carry me away and disappear, then reappear in the middle of the field beyond Jeffrey's house, the sun cresting the horizon line.

The rage takes over, pounds at my chest.

I can't do this without him.

I don't want to.

How do I fix him?

How the fuck do I have all of this power and can't figure out how to fucking fix him?

Fuck!

Hands balled at my sides, I tip my head toward the sky and scream. I scream and scream and scream.

The ground shakes.

Energy builds in the air, electric on my skin and I can't contain it. I don't want to. I want the world to burn.

Light flashes across the clearing and then—

BOOM.

Power leaves me in a blast, rippling outward.

The pines bow, the trunks snap, and the forest topples like dominos.

Dust and dirt plumes in the air and I collapse to my knees, breathing heavy.

I fold into myself and sob.

What is this? What does it all mean? I'm terrified of who I am and what I am and what I can do and—

"*Dieva*."

I go still and my heart seizes in my chest.

I can hear his footsteps on the brittle grass. Can hear the steady rush of blood in his veins.

Please don't be an illusion.

Tears stream down my face when I turn and look over my shoulder.

He stands in a patch of field grass, the sunlight burnishing him in gold.

He's alive.

He's alive.

I climb to my feet and race across the field and he opens his arms for me.

When I crash into him, he grunts, and wraps me into him, tightens his hold on me, buries his face in my hair and inhales.

"*Dieva*," he starts.

"How did...how are you okay?"

"You, I assume," he says. "And whatever power you just unleashed."

"But I don't know how—" Does it matter though? Maybe it doesn't. He's here and he's alive and—

"Why did you do it? Why did you step in front of me?"

He cradles my head against him. "You wish to torture me further?"

"Please."

He sighs with a ragged breath, then puts his hands on either side of my face and pulls me back. "I had already lost everything and the only thing I had left"—he meets my gaze, the flecks of white-gray flashing in the early morning light—"was you."

The tears well in my eyes again and Wrath pulls his thumb over my cheek, wiping them away.

"*Dieva*," he scolds.

"I love you."

He frowns at me, as if this is the most unfortunate turn of events.

"You don't have to say it. But I know you love me too. I know you love me the only way you can and I'm telling you right now, it's enough. If you're willing to look past the fact that I stole all of your power, I want you in every—"

He kisses me.

He kisses me as the sun bakes us and burns the mist from the ground.

He kisses me, not with gentle hands, but with fierce conviction.

And I hear him in that kiss.

I hear him like a resounding thunderclap.

I love you too.

CHAPTER
NINETEEN

For most of my life, I wanted to be talented like my mother. At her events, I'd watch people stare at her work and get lost in it, marvel at the light and the color and the mood. It was just pixels in a camera, an image later printed on paper, but what my mother created through her camera wasn't just a picture, it was a feeling.

Studying Mom and how she worked, I could mimic what she did. I knew how to find the light, how to turn down the aperture to get that gorgeous bokeh. But I didn't know how to put feeling into an image.

I didn't know how to love a subject the way my mother loved the mist on the Cliffs of Moher or the cloud cover in a mountain range. I never connected with those things. They didn't move me.

It wasn't until I took those pictures of Wrath that I finally *knew*.

I knew what it was to be moved by something and it terrified me.

I'd been chasing a dream and once I was living it, it became too fucking real.

And Wrath...

He had always been terrified of being powerless.

And now, as we stand surrounded by the wreckage of the forest, we have both been laid bare.

I look up at him as the sharpness of the sunlight gives way to the cloud cover. "I can probably give it back to you," I tell him. "The *dominus* and the *oculus* and—"

He shakes his head and spins me around so we face the blast zone. "Look at this."

"I am," I say, a little embarrassed. This takes a tantrum to a whole new level.

"I've never done anything like this," he says.

"What? But—"

"I wanted to prove to you over and over again that I was more powerful than you. But deep down, I knew that wasn't true. I could feel it. I think I felt it the first moment I crossed paths with you in the alley."

I look up at him. "Sirene believes I'm a reincarnated goddess. That I'm—"

"Reignyabit." He tightens his hold on me, draws me in. "I pretended that your name didn't set off alarm bells in my head, and then when your mother admitted that Sirene had a hand in naming you—" He sighs and turns us, walking us back to the house.

"Do you think it's true?" My heart hammers in my head waiting for his answer.

"Yes."

"But—"

"You just destroyed a forest."

"Yes, but—"

"No more buts. The sooner you embrace it, the quicker we can defeat my brother."

"Are we still doing that?"

"Do you want him to take your throne?"

I roll my eyes as we crest the hill and the field grass turns into packed gravel around the house. "I'm not taking your throne."

"Someone has to. It better be you."

We come to a stop beside the house's front porch. A hummingbird zigzags around a red feeder at the end of the roofline. When I focus my gaze on it, I can see its wings, the quick beat of them as if time has slowed.

I quickly look away.

I think I might still be terrified of what this all means. Of the power that now runs through my veins.

"I think General Briggs is looking for a way to cross over to Alius."

Wrath's gaze fixes on a point beyond the top of my head. "Of course he is." His eyes narrow and flash red. "Chaos will be looking for a way to leverage that greed. And Briggs will be looking for a way to turn Chaos's ambition into a tool. But both of them lack one thing."

"What's that?"

"You."

"I don't want the throne."

"As you keep reminding me and yet you have the Demon King's power."

But do I? Or do I have what belonged to the goddess? It's ludicrous to believe a myth is now my reality. So maybe I won't look at it too closely.

Not yet anyway.

"Tell me what you loved about being king."

He frowns at me. "We don't have time for this—"

"Tell me."

He sighs again. "I suppose I'll have to get used to you demanding things of me and me being powerless to deny you."

"I could get used to it. Now answer the question."

"Being king was a great honor and I meant to take it seriously in the beginning. But the longer I was king, the more I realized I would always be used for something, and when I wasn't being used, I would be plotted against and betrayed.

"I had to be more powerful. More ruthless. In the end, I held onto my power with a firm grip because it was the only thing that never stabbed me in the back."

"I plotted against you," I say. "I betrayed you."

"Yes, but the difference between you and those who came before you? You never did it for power. You were just a soaking wet puppy pedaling to stay above water."

"Hey!" I give him a playful shove and he catches me by the wrist easily enough, wrangling me into him. I maybe have the triad now, but he is still twice as big as me. "And now what am I?"

He glances at me. "Still a thorn in my side, surely."

"And you're still just as cantankerous."

A hint of a smile lifts the corner of his mouth and then, "Why did you come back?"

"What?"

"You came to the stables. To me."

How do I sum it all up? I left Gus on a mission to declare my love to Wrath, but I had no clue how I was going to declare it.

We've been through so much; we've fought each other around every corner.

We may not be connected any longer, but I can feel him just the same and something has irrevocably changed in him and in me.

"Like you, I've always felt alone," I tell him. "In different ways, for different reasons, but I realized that when I'm with you, I don't feel that way. I don't *want* to be alone."

He looks down at me, eyes squinted against the light, his

hand wrapped around my wrist. "I still stand by by my earlier warning," he says. "I will not love you gently."

"I know." I let power surge to my arm and it zaps him with heat. He snaps his hand back and shakes out the pain. "And I will not bend easily."

"Perhaps we were made for each other after all, *dieva*."

I think of the story of the dark god and the bright goddess.

"Maybe we were."

"Now," he says, "let's go plot a war, shall we?"

I hold out my hand to him and he takes it without hesitation even though I just burned him. "To the war, daddy."

He grumbles as he pulls me from the clearing.

TWENTY

We find Mom and Jeffrey in the cabin's kitchen.

"Feeling better, Wrath?" Mom asks.

"I am." He gives them each a curt nod. "I am grateful for your help."

"Of course." Jeffrey sets his cup down. "You two want a cup of coffee? I'm having mine spiked if you want to join me."

"We have to go, actually."

Before coming back inside, Wrath and I came up with a plan. It starts with visiting Rhys and his house.

"Baby, so soon?" Mom frowns at me, long, dangly earrings swinging from her ears. She's changed clothes, since hers were covered in the Demon King's blood. Which means she has a bag here, which means she was planning to stay. I'm not going to pry, but knowing Mom has reconnected with the man she thought of as my biological father for most of my life makes my chest warm.

"We have some stuff we have to deal with," I tell her.

"Something to do with the Demon King getting shot full of bullets, I'm guessing?" Jeffrey says.

"You would be correct in that assumption," Wrath answers.

"Rainy baby." Mom comes forward, her drapey ruana tucked closed beneath her folded arms. "I'm worried about you and the big guy. He didn't look too good when you just popped up here out of thin air. You never did tell us what happened. What is going on?"

"Ms. Low," Wrath says, "I can assure you, Rain is capable of handling herself."

"I know. She always has been, but—" She frowns at me, then reaches over and squeezes my arm. "I know you've always been able to take care of yourself, but I've been worried about you. I just want you to know that."

"I know, Mom." I wrap my arms around her neck and give her a long hug and as we're locked together, I hear her thoughts.

My baby doesn't need me anymore. Not that she ever did. Never needed me like I thought a child would. Always older than her years.

I'm not going to cry again.

I inhale deeply, memorizing all of the layers of her scent. Patchouli. Lavender. Herbal tea. Tea tree oil. Coffee and weed. I'm immediately settled by the familiarity.

Maybe I haven't given my mother enough credit over the years. She was a hands-off parent, but I never asked her for help. I never asked her to come home. I always kept her at a distance. "I'll be okay. I promise."

She kisses my cheek. "I know."

When we step back, Wrath takes my hand in his.

"You still owe me a cup of tea, Ms. Low," Wrath says. "Perhaps I'll take that promise next time we cross paths."

"I'd like that." She smiles up at him. "Bye, baby. Call me when you can."

"I will." I give Jeffrey a nod before my newfound power pulls us away.

~

RHYS SEEMS to be expecting us. He and the others are assembled in their main living room with another dozen vampires spread throughout.

And I spot Lauren and Arthur there too.

I'm immediately relieved to see them both alive and well. Even Lauren.

I rush over to her and wrap her in a hug and she goes rigid in my grasp. "What the hell are you doing?"

"I'm glad you're okay."

"Okayyyyy."

When I let her go, I find her frowning at me and fighting a snarl. "We can hate each other all day long, but I don't want you dead," I say.

The snarl softens, but she crosses her arms over her chest. "I suppose I could say the same. Right now, that is. Not a few days ago. A few days ago I wanted you dead. Tomorrow...probably also the same."

Wrath has always been searching for loyalty only for people to disappoint him. Lauren has always been by his side. She's earned her spot and I won't take it away from her.

"Arthur." I'm gentle with my hug for him. He's holding up well, but I can hear his thoughts like a distant buzz in the back of my head. *Hurts. Hurts. Hurts.*

He hugs me back, pats me affectionately. "I'm glad you're okay, Rain."

"How are you?"

"I'm good."

If Wrath was able to help with the pain, could I now that I have the triad? I've been given the launch controls to a rocket ship but I don't know which buttons to push. Wrath might have taught me how to control the *animus*, but I think there's more to it now.

And anyway, I'm different than Wrath.

I have to embrace that if I'm to get anywhere.

And finally accepting that fact, that I am something other than human, but something other than Wrath, is almost like a briar finally pulling loose.

There's instant relief.

I take Arthur's hand and instead of pushing out with the power, I pull in. We're in the far corner of the room, shadowed by heavy drapes and low lighting, so when I start glowing, it's immediately noticeable.

The room goes quiet behind me and Arthur's eyes widen before his face goes slack, all of the tension leaving the fine, aged lines around his mouth.

I hear his thoughts ease out.

Better. So much better. All the pain gone.

When I let him go and step back, he sighs. "Wow. Rain. Thank you. I haven't felt this great in a very long time."

"I'm glad to hear that."

He stretches, rolls his shoulders. "In fact, I think you healed me."

"For now," I say. "Just like Wrath."

"No." He shakes his head. "This is different." His eyes are glassy and his Adam's apple bobs on a hard swallow. "Thank you. Truly."

"I didn't...I mean..."

He wraps me in a hug, squeezing me with renewed strength and I can't help it—I get a little teary-eyed too.

I don't know if I healed him entirely, but any sign of relief is a good thing.

When Arthur lets me go, I turn to the room and everyone immediately looks at my chest. For a hot second, I wonder if

I've burned away my t-shirt and bra and am flashing the room.

But when I look down, I find a demon mark, not unlike Wrath's, glowing almost phosphorescent beneath my skin.

And on the next breath, it disappears entirely.

"Whoa. What is that?" I can't hide the panicked edge to my voice. "Does that mean I'm a demon now?"

I don't know that I necessarily want to be a demon.

Wrath comes to my side. "Where you are concerned, *dieva*, everything is a mystery. We'll learn as we go."

I smile over at him, so fucking grateful to have him by my side while I figure this shit out.

"Wrath." Rhys comes forward. "We should discuss our strategy before they get ahead of us."

I frown. "Before who gets ahead of us?"

There's a look shared between Rhys and Wrath. A look that says, *Are we letting the girl sit at the table?*

Steeling my spine, I step in front of Wrath and say to the gorgeous, slightly scary vampire, "I can read your mind if I need to. So I suggest you just tell me instead of going about it the hard way."

He narrows his eyes, lip curling back as if he means to bare his fangs at me.

Truth be told, I'm bullshitting on the mind-reading thing. I might be able to read his mind. I really don't know. I can't hear anything right this second. But like Wrath says, everything about me is a mystery and Rhys Roman doesn't know if I can or can't read his mind. Something tells me he's not the betting type. He wouldn't have a massive estate house like this if he was.

Wrath, for his part, keeps his mouth shut, watching.

I sense his pride in me and it makes me fucking glow.

"Chaos has found a way into Last Vale and he and the

United States Government are currently assembling outside my city's perimeter and intend to infiltrate it," Rhys explains.

Well. That's not good.

"The ley line," I say, remembering what Wrath told me before. "You think they're getting ready to open a portal to Alius?"

"I would assume that's precisely what they're planning on doing," Wrath answers.

"How do we stop him?"

Rhys gestures to the rest of the vampires gathered around the room. Most of them are in pockets of conversation, their voices low as they wait for orders. "These are my sentinels," Rhys says. "They're ready to move when I give the word. I have another dozen vampires at my call."

I look at Wrath. "Do you still have the army you were building? The one I saw in the castle?"

"I've lost some of the norrow." His expression is blank, emotionless, but I think it kills him to admit it. "I still have an entire army of demons."

"What about the witches?"

Overhearing the mention of her kind, Kat pipes in, "Any witch we could have called an ally is deathly afraid of being exposed."

Dane hangs his head over the back of the sofa to add, "You may or may not know this, but last time witches were exposed, they were burned at the stake. Witch-kabobs around every corner."

"Hey, asshole!" Kat makes a move to slap him upside the back of the head, but he catches her by the wrist and laughs.

"Okay, so with those numbers, do we have a chance? I mean...vampires and demons up against a mortal military. That shouldn't be a big deal, right?"

"Normally, no," Rhys says.

"Why do I get the impression this is not a 'normally' situation?"

He cants his head and a lock of his dirty blond hair falls out of place over his forehead. "The other witches, the ones we don't count as allies? They're quite all right with being exposed. And I've got word they've aligned with Chaos and the president."

"Why would they do that?"

"Because they hate me and they want Last Vale."

I grimace. I don't know much about magic, but I guess a town that sits over a powerful ley line must be something to covet.

"How long do you think we have?"

"Not long," Wrath surmises.

"So what do we—" I cut myself off when I feel a distant tugging and a whisper inside my head.

Wrath angles his body toward me as if he means to jump in front of me, shield me from whatever might be wrong. "What is it?"

"Something is calling on me."

"In what way?"

Rain. Come bargain with me.

"It's Chaos," I answer.

Wrath scowls and drops his arms, hands fisted at his side. "How is he speaking to you?"

"I don't—" I feel the tug again and know right away where he is. "He's at Reignyabit's *porta lima.*"

"What is that?" Rhys asks.

Wrath is looking at me when he answers. "A place of worship for the goddess Reignyabit."

"I told you," Kat tells Dane.

"Just because she feels some phantom belly poking doesn't mean she's an actual goddess," Dane argues.

167

Wrath is still pinning me with his gaze. "I think that's exactly what it means."

"I need to go to him."

Wrath lashes out and grabs me by the arm. "No, you don't."

"Yes, I do."

"*Dieva.*"

I get in close to him and lower my voice, even though it won't do much good in a room full of vampires. "Do you trust me?"

He takes in a deep breath, nostrils flaring as his jaw flexes. "Yes."

"Then let me do this."

"It's my brother I don't trust."

"If I'm really a goddess, then it won't matter what he does."

Again with the bullshit, but a girl has to do what a girl has to do. Even ones pretending to be goddesses.

"What do you plan to say to him?" Wrath drops my arm and hunches closer, bringing his face level with mine. "What could this possibly accomplish, *dieva*?"

"An opportunity to bargain with him before people die."

He scoffs. "Casualties of war are to be expected."

I look at Rhys. "Is that what you want for your vampires? Just to be casualties?"

"Obviously not."

"So let me talk to him first. See if we can find a better way."

"You're wasting your time," Wrath says with a growl.

"I'll be back soon."

He grits his teeth, then, "Be careful."

"I will," I promise.

CHAPTER
TWENTY-ONE

I find Chaos in the mausoleum that is supposedly dedicated to worshipping me in a former life.

If someone was to worship me now, they would be dealt a healthy dose of disillusionment. I barely have my own life together, let alone the ability to bless someone else's.

Chaos stands at the stone gateway, hands clasped behind his back. When he hears me appear, he turns just slightly, his face coming into profile. He's wearing his glasses again and a navy-blue cardigan over a white and blue plaid button-up.

He certainly looks better than the last time I saw him.

"What do you want, Chaos?"

"I wasn't so sure you'd come. I wasn't so sure you'd hear the call. Looks like I was wrong on both counts."

I know what he's insinuating—he's as surprised as I am to be given further proof that I'm Reignyabit.

"I'm here. So tell me what you want."

He finally turns to me and comes down the three steps from the dais in front of the gate. "We haven't really had a chance to speak alone."

I scan the rest of the mausoleum. It's only one room, but

there's an open corridor that circles the sunken center and plenty of stone columns and tangled vines for someone to hide behind.

"I'm listening."

"You're different than the last time I saw you." He starts to circle me. "Did you take the last of the triad?"

I cross my arms over my chest. "Did I take it? No."

Technically true. I didn't intend to take it.

"But you have it just the same."

"Yes."

He nods, continues to pace around me. "Maybe Sirene and Ciri were right after all. And if they were right—" He comes to a halt. "You have no idea how much power runs through your veins or what you could do with that power."

"Tell me. It sounds like you have it all planned out."

"We could rule Alius together."

"Power was never a thing I wanted."

"What *do* you want then?"

"I don't know. What does every girl want? A pumpkin spice latte and a good book to curl up with?"

He snorts. "You're funnier than I would have expected."

"And you're not as tall as I would have expected."

He laughs, keeps circling.

"Join me."

"No."

"Why?"

"Because—"

"Because you think you love him." He sighs. "Lots of women, and men, think they love him. You go to Alius with him, you'll be fighting them off every single day. He will never be yours. Not entirely." The line of his jaw hardens. "My brother has always been adored, even when he's at his worst."

"It sounds like you're jealous of him."

Chaos laughs. "Are you surprised? I did try to take his throne, after all." He keeps walking. "Did you know I was betrothed?"

"Yes."

"Do you know he killed her?"

I swallow, take a breath. "Yes."

"And yet you would still follow him into war? Spend your life in his bed?"

I pivot to keep him in front of me. "I know he's done terrible things. I know who he is, Chaos. He's the villain, and I love him."

He nods, slows his pace. "Nothing will change your mind?"

"No."

There is the distinct sound of stone grinding over stone through the vines. A second later, the vines pull back and the president of the United States walks in. And she's not alone.

She has my mother in tow.

~

"What the fuck?"

"I'm sorry, baby," Mom says. "When the president called and invited me to tea, what was I supposed to say?"

"*No*, Mom! You were supposed to say no!"

She clasps her hands together. "I'm sorry." She lowers her voice like she's telling me a secret. "It's Naomi Wright! You know how I feel about Naomi Wright!"

The President comes forward. She's wearing her usual blue blazer, tailored chinos, and pearl necklace. She is the picture of perfection while clearly on the verge of threatening my mother for my cooperation.

I know this because I can hear the buzz of her thoughts like an annoying gnat in my ear.

"Now before you get brave," Naomi says, "and use your power to poof out of here—go on, Sunny."

Mom's thoughts start bouncing around in her head.

Unfortunate position I've put us in. I hope my baby will forgive me. I hope she'll get out of this all right.

And beneath that, a strong current of fear as she pulls open the drapey front of her ruana to reveal a vest that appears to be rigged with wires.

"A bomb," Naomi says. "I don't have the detonator, but rest assured, we could trigger it within seconds."

Fear spikes through me and my stomach drops.

When I look back at Mom, she's got her arms spread, shoulders hunched in a shrug like, *What are ya gonna do?*

But in her mind, she's thinking one thing: *I'm sorry, baby.*

"I respected you," I tell Naomi. "I liked you even. I thought you were one of the good ones."

"I am. But sometimes even the good ones have to do unfortunate things in order to accomplish what is, ultimately, the right thing."

"Which is what? Infiltrate another world?"

"We need cooperation, between us and Chaos. He can help us stabilize our country and—"

"Steal a throne."

"No. We don't want the throne."

I snort.

"Think about it Rain. Now that the world knows another world exists? It'll be a race to infiltrate it, control it," Naomi goes on. "It'll be the lunar landing all over again. But I promise you, not all of those who desire to cross over will have honorable plans. There are men like Ryder and MAW who would love to go rogue in a new world."

"What do you want me for?" I ask.

"Chaos informs me you hold the power that would control the throne."

"I guess."

"It only makes sense to have you on our side."

"Except that will never happen."

Naomi puts her arm around Mom's shoulder. "I'd like you to reconsider that, Rain."

Mom presses a hand to her chest, eyebrows drawn together.

What the hell am I to do?

Pick between Wrath and my mother?

"Do you have a way through?" I ask.

Naomi looks me dead in the eyes. "Half of a way."

Her thoughts confirm that.

They have a traveler but they need me and my blood to finish opening it, just like Sirene and Ciri did.

Fucking fuckery.

I turn away from them, hands on my hips as I think. I've never been one for strategic thinking. I'm an action kind of girl. Boots on the ground, get the work done.

I don't have very many options. Would they hurt Mom if I left here now so I could regroup with Wrath and figure out a way to rescue her? Something tells me that Naomi might be more vicious than I gave her credit for and General Briggs would probably torture a schoolteacher if it got him what he wanted.

I can't use the sub-dimension to transport us out of here. Not with a bomb strapped to Mom's chest.

The more I analyze it, the worse my options look.

I pace to the gateway and look up at Reignyabit's symbol— the blazing sun.

Help me, I think to her. *If I'm really you, help me figure this shit out.*

I'm sure an ancient goddess can appreciate twenty-first century cussing, right?

Hello Bright Goddess! Is anyone listening?

Of course there isn't.

I'm almost ready to give up when warmth spreads through my body and the first thread of an idea comes to me.

It has no shape yet. It's just a shadow growing long on the wall.

But it springs hope at the center of me and I need more time to work out the details.

I need to stall them. I'm not usually a liar, but desperate times call for shady tactics.

"Okay," I say and turn back to them.

"Okay?" Naomi lifts a razor-sharp brow.

"I'll help you," I answer. "In exchange for my mother's safety, I'll help you get what you want."

CHAPTER
TWENTY-TWO

Naomi takes my mother away and promises she'll be safe—for now.

Chaos and I go to Saint Sabine to a desolate street that curves uphill and is surrounded on both sides by woods.

I can't recall ever coming to this part of town.

On a deep inhale, I smell the distinct smells of the Second Quarter to the north—gumbo and the fish market and sweet tobacco.

Judging by the aromas and the faint din of the city, I don't think we're more than a mile away from the Second, but it feels like another state.

There's something indistinct about this street, something quietly unnoticeable.

"Here?" I ask.

Chaos nods and starts forward on a dirt path through the woods.

When I step through the hollow between bramble bushes, Sirene appears out of the mist. She's wearing all black. There's thick leather ribbing around her shoulders and her torso. Knives strapped to her forearms. Two more around each thigh.

Her blonde hair is braided along the crown and tied into a tight ponytail at the back of her head.

She is a vision of a warrior queen.

At this point in our relationship, I'm never sure if I should be thanking Sirene or strangling her.

"Take her to the field," Chaos instructs. "When we get through, take her to the gate in Last Vale."

"Where are you going?" I ask him. I need to know where everyone is if I'm going to plot an escape.

"I have to go back for Naomi and your mother."

Don't react to that news.

The closer Mom is to me, the easier it'll be to poof her out of here when the time is right.

Chaos gives Sirene a quick nod and then disappears.

"So that ability, traveling through the sub-dimension, who has it?"

"Just the royal line," Sirene answers. "Wrath, Chaos, the princes, and the lords. The rest of the demons have to use the power of their own two legs."

"And now me," I say.

She looks over at me with a glint of pride in her eyes. "Yes, and now you."

We start walking, following the trodden dirt path as it winds through the misty forest as night descends around us.

"I can't believe you haven't murdered him yet."

"Chaos?" she asks and continues before I've confirmed it. "He's just a means to an end. He wanted to think otherwise, but he's never been able to see the world beyond the end of his own nose."

"Don't you feel bad using him?"

"No. He doesn't feel bad using you."

She has an excellent point.

"So, exactly which side are you on?"

She's behind me on the path, her footsteps quiet.

"I'm on your side."

I snort. "That's the biggest line of bullshit."

"Ciri and I had a plan and the plan was always you. Some elements of the plan were not fun and will not be fun, not for you. But we do have an end goal."

I stop in the path to glance at her over my shoulder. "Which is what?"

She stops too, face blank.

"Am I meant to succeed or fail in your master plan?"

"That's entirely up to you. Ciri always made it clear to me that we could only set things in motion. We were not to influence them."

I snort. "So make me a cog in your elegant machine. I see."

"Or," she says, "maybe you're the machine and we're all the cogs clicking into place."

"You really think I'm a goddess?"

"I think you're the better version of Wrath."

The light to his dark. Just like the stones Kat made for our binding spell. One white. One dark.

I think back to the myth, the Dark Father God, the Bright Goddess.

The shadow of an idea takes on more shape.

A thought prickles along my subconscious.

Dark and light. Light and dark.

Two halves of a whole.

Butterflies fill my stomach.

I keep walking, ignoring the shiver that wracks my shoulders.

❧

WHEN THE WOODS open up to a field, we come to a stop. Not because of the change in scenery, but because of the soldiers.

The military is lined up on the edge of the field dressed in army fatigues, massive guns in hand. I don't know their numbers but I'd guess there are easily five hundred men and women.

And at the other end of the field is Wrath and Rhys and Kat and an army of demons and vampires.

Wrath spots me and his eyes narrow.

He's devastatingly handsome in the shifting light of torches and spotlights.

He's wearing armor I've never seen before. All black leather and black metal with reticulated plates over his shoulders, and leather straps that run across his torso.

There are blades strapped to his back. Not that the Demon King needs them.

Even without the triad, I suspect he's more than most of us can handle.

It's why he had the triad in the first place.

When we lock eyes, I push one singular thought to him: *Please trust me.*

I have not betrayed him.

I *won't* betray him.

Beyond Wrath and his army sits a sprawling town nestled between the field and the ocean. I immediately smell the salty sea air, can hear the waves crashing against the rocks.

On the edge of a cliff, a massive estate house overlooks both the town and the ocean, but its windows are dark. In fact, most of the buildings seem to be settled in a state of waiting.

I don't know where the gate is here, but I can feel the massive pulse of the ley line.

The energy of it ripples along my skin, lifting the air along my arms.

"This place literally beats with magic," I say.

Sirene nods. "That's why everyone wants it and the world that lies beyond it."

As if on cue, Naomi's soldiers are joined by men and women dressed in street clothes. Not soldiers, but witches.

The air grows charged with the promise of violence.

I might be in over my head.

What the hell am I going to do?

I scan the crowd for Naomi and my mother but don't spot them. How far away will they be?

I look at Wrath again and find his eyes glowing red, his face growing sharper as the demon king comes out to play.

If he doesn't trust me, he'll likely be plotting my death right about now.

If only the connection was still open between us, I could tell him...

"Now what?" I say to Sirene.

She shrugs, clasps her hands behind her back. "I'm not running this show."

The air settles and almost as if the world senses the building promise of war, the waves quiet, the sea grows still.

A breeze crosses the field rattling the grass and lifting the hair from around my face.

"You can turn back now," Wrath calls, his voice booming in the clearing. "Or you can die soon enough."

Several yards to my left, the soldiers part and Chaos walks through.

Where's my mother? Where's Naomi? Fuck.

A cold sweat breaks out along my spine.

"We both know you've grown weak, brother." Chaos stops at the head of the assembled army. He's still in his cardigan and looks painfully out of place among the army fatigues. "I think it's time you retire. You've had the throne long enough and now you no longer possess the power to rule it."

Chaos cuts his gaze to me and Wrath follows it.

Both demon brothers pin me with their heavy stares and my skin crawls.

I backpedal, but Sirene is behind me, and I bump into her.

"I don't like this," I say to her. "This is going to be a bloodbath."

"And I wonder," she says to me, "what will the goddess do?"

The knowing burning through my veins solidifies.

Come on, Rain.

If you're a goddess, you can figure this out.

Light and Dark. Night and Day. God and Goddess.

Yes, that's it.

God and Goddess.

It was never one or the other.

The thought comes into clearer focus, the outline taking shape.

I'm grasping at straws, but that's all I have right now.

"Let us delay this no longer," Chaos says.

And all hell breaks loose.

TWENTY-THREE

Bullets start flying immediately and the smell of blood fills the air. The witches stay nestled amongst the soldiers and begin chanting in unison.

That can't be good.

That can't be good at all.

"What are they doing?" I ask Sirene.

"What they do best."

"Which is what?"

"Shielding the soldiers and weakening the enemy."

Several vampires go down across the clearing and immediately burst into ash.

Sirene's mouth drops open. "They're using wooden bullets," she says. "They're smarter than I gave them credit for."

Kat is on the other side. And Rhys and Dane. As annoying as he is, I don't want him to die. And Emery...if she lost Rhys...

If I'm going to do this, I have to do it now.

I pull on my power and my hair flutters around my face.

Sirene turns to me. "Where do you think you're going?"

"I'm sorry, Sirene. I already picked my side and it isn't this one."

She frowns at me and for a second, I think she still sees me as that fat, wailing baby making a fuss.

Before she can respond, I disappear and pop back up on the other side of the clearing right in front of Wrath.

"I can't wait to hear your excuse this time," he says.

"They have my mom," I tell him and his face falls.

"They have Sunny?"

More bullets fly through the air. Someone screams and then a gust of wind shoots across the field kicking up dirt, forcing some of the vampires to fall back. Witches, probably.

We're running out of time.

Heart racing, I grab him by the arm and yank us from the field and deposit us hundreds of miles away in the belly of the castle.

Water drips somewhere in the background and the air smells like charred wood.

Wrath looks around. "Why bring us here?"

"We're going to lose."

He frowns at me. "I don't run from war."

"I don't want to run *or* lose. I want my mom back. They have her tethered to a bomb."

There is a noticeable rumble deep in his chest. "I'll make them regret threatening Sunny. You have my word."

It's almost endearing hearing the Demon King promise revenge for my mother.

"I appreciate that, but...we need a better plan than the one we've got."

"If you have one, *dieva*, I'm open to hearing it, but be quick with it."

I move past him and start searching the stone floor.

"I'll admit, this isn't quite what I thought you had in mind," he says.

"Shhh. I'm looking for something."

"On the floor?"

I finally spot it, the rock from my favorite game of Reach for the Rock.

Plucking it from the floor, the rock is cool in my grasp, sharp on its backside.

Turning to Wrath, I find him with his arms crossed eyeing me warily.

"I've been thinking about the myth, the one about the Dark Father God and the Bright Goddess. The Dark God was jealous of the goddess. Do you remember?"

"Yes. I know the story."

"The Dark God didn't want to believe that they were equals so he stole the goddess's power."

His face darkens. He and I both see the similarities between the story and the way he regarded me when he realized I had the *animus*.

He didn't want to believe we were on any equal standing.

But I think we've moved beyond that.

I have to believe we have.

"The Dark God broke the power into three pieces," I go on. "Because it's much harder to be equal when there are three parts."

"What are you getting at?"

Excitement drums in my chest.

Please let this work.

"They were Night and Day, darkness and light," I say. "Two halves. They were always supposed to *share* the power."

Palm flat, I hold out the rock. I don't know what I'm doing. It's like I've walked into an advanced calculus class with nothing more than a strong wish and desire to make the math work.

It has to work.

I have faith it will. I can feel the surety of it rushing through my veins.

"What do you plan to do?" Wrath asks, narrowing his eyes at me.

I close my fingers around the stone and the sharp side slices through my palm, blood immediately welling in my grasp. Heat cascades down my arm and pools in my fingertips. The beat of the power is like a war drum and the harder it beats, the more I believe in it.

The rock heats up and glows in the cage of my fingers.

Wrath unfolds his arms, eyes widening.

Focusing on the stone, I put my heart into what I want for it, knowing that it isn't the stone so much as it is the *desire*.

I never wanted the power in the first place and Wrath wanted it so badly, he lost it.

But I'm not the light without the dark. And he is not the dark without the light.

I don't want to do it alone.

Without *my* dark god by my side.

When the light cuts out a second later, and I open my hand, the slick, black stone has been etched with runes.

"It was always meant to be us," I say. "We've been fighting each other this entire time, terrified of what this was, deep down knowing that it was *something*. I don't want to do this alone. And I don't think I'm meant to." I hold out my hand. "Take it."

He frowns at my palm, then regards me with cool detachment. "You would so easily give up your power?"

"Half of it. But yes. *For you*, yes."

I don't even have to think about it. And neither does he.

Without hesitation, he reaches over and slides his hand into mine, covering the rock.

The second our skin touches, both connected to the rock,

the light returns, but this time it shoots across the cavern like the swirling light of a lighthouse.

The castle foundation rocks and the floor cracks and Wrath puts his hand on the wall to hold himself steady as he's remade.

Remade into something new.

A dark god and a bright goddess.

Two halves of a whole.

Night and Day.

The light flickers like flame, then pulls up his arm, winds around his chest, and glows in his eyes before it settles along the edges of his dark demon mark.

When the light dies out a second later, Wrath is breathing heavily. He nods at my chest.

I look down to see my phosphorescent mark glowing beneath my skin, now outlined in black.

It worked. It fucking worked.

And even better, I can feel him again.

The connection thrums strongly between us and through that connection, I let him know exactly how I feel.

I love him and I trust him and I made my decision—I want to always be by his side.

He gives me the smallest of nods, acknowledging what he feels echoing through the connection.

"I don't know how to use the power," I admit to him. "Not like you do."

He holds out his hand to me. "I'll teach you as much as I can."

"You have a deal."

How can you not believe in gods and goddesses when you've met demons and witches and vampires?

How can you not believe in ancient myths when they come true right before your eyes?

We were always meant for this. Ciri knew it. Sirene knew it.

The darkness and the moon. The sun and the shadows.

Night and Day.

One is never meant to exist without the other.

"Now let's go kick some ass," I say.

Wrath gives me a nod. "Let's rescue your mother. She owes me a cup of tea, after all."

The simple mention of the tea brings tears to my eyes and I think I fall in love with this man, the *villain*, all over again.

CHAPTER
TWENTY-FOUR

When we reappear, it's pandemonium.

"About fucking time," Rhys says to my left.

Blood is smeared over his mouth, drips down his chin and his eyes are glowing in the dim light.

"We're getting our asses kicked," he shouts as a loud boom goes off and three vampires are thrown back.

They're throwing grenades.

Wrath looks down at me. "Are you ready?"

"With you by my side, abso-fucking-lutely."

"That mouth of yours, *dieva*," he says and lets the thought hang in the air. I know what he means and smile up at him.

"Do you feel any different?" I ask. "Can we win?"

He nods. "Somehow I feel more power than before."

I feel it too. It's this surety at my core. We are somehow greater than our individual parts. I feel unstoppable right now. I don't know if it's true or not, but I'm willing to have faith if it means getting my mother to safety.

"Come," he says, "and let us have our retribution."

My own mark lights up with the thrill.

Wrath and I surge forward into the field.

I'VE NEVER REALLY FOUGHT for anything in my life.

I had opinions, ones I made sure everyone else knew too.

But I never put action behind those beliefs, never risked life and limb.

When Wrath and I cross the field, my heart beats loudly in my ears as the blood pumps fast through my veins.

We don't speak, don't strategize. Somehow we know what to do. It's a feeling that needs no words.

He lifts his arm and the darkness kicks up like a tidal wave, then crashes down through the assembled army. They're scattered like tin soldiers.

The fire builds up inside of me and the darkness burns away as I take several steps.

The witches come forward, mouths moving in their chant, then one throws her arms out and bright light shoots out from her hands.

My power flares into a shield and the hit bounces off.

The witches have no idea what they've gotten themselves into.

I pull the shield down and throw my arms out.

Fire rages across the clearing then ignites in a towering blast when it reaches the assembled troops. Several witches drop, engulfed in flames.

To my right, Wrath disappears and reappears behind the enemy's line. Shouting erupts as they realize he's in their midst, but they aren't fast enough to pivot. His darkness shoots out like an arrow, piercing several of the soldiers. They go down, blood painting the air.

I'm not a vicious person—I'm no villain—but there is a beat of something vicious-like at my sternum, a building crescendo, a whisper of something darker and older and it says:

You will not fuck with what's mine. You will not fuck with those I love.

You will pay for this.

I never considered myself powerful but, in this moment, I am swept up in it, in being invincible.

In this moment, I believe.

I will reign.

I am Reign.

And these motherfuckers are about to learn.

CHAPTER
TWENTY-FIVE

THE CARNAGE PAINTS THE NIGHT IN SHADES OF FIRE AND BLOOD.

It doesn't take Wrath and me long to make our way through the enemy line and once bodies start dropping, whoever is in charge calls for the rest to fall back. They scatter like dry leaves. Even the witches.

Rhys and Kat and Dane come up behind us. The vampires are covered in blood, their eyes bright with a predatory glow.

Kat is breathing heavily, but the smile on her face is wide. "Those witches bit off more than they could chew," she says.

"We should pay them a visit after all of this," Dane suggests. "Really drive home our point."

"There will be plenty of time for that." Rhys drags the back of his knuckles over his chin, wiping away more blood. "You need anything further from us?"

I have to find my mom, but I don't think we need the vampires for that.

Wrath must sense my thoughts. "I think we'll tackle this one alone. Take care of your people."

Rhys nods. "If you need me, you know how to find me."

They head down the field, the moonlight painting them in an outline of silver.

"Before I gave you half the power," I tell Wrath, "I could sense people. I did it when Ryder and MAW took me. There was this casting, like a net, and anyone within its reach popped up on my awareness like a buoy in the water. Did you ever feel that?"

"Before I lost the triad? No. Now..." He turns his attention beyond us, his eyes narrowing. "Things are different now. This is new territory for both of us, apparently."

"But we'll figure it out together. Right?"

His gaze cuts back to me. "Of course, *dieva*."

"I can still sense people, I'm realizing, but I don't sense my mother near. And I wonder if the net isn't big enough, if we're going to continue on that analogy."

"Perhaps we need both of us." He offers me his hand. My heart kicks up just at the mere thought of touching him and he must catch it, because the corner of his mouth lifts in a smug, knowing smile.

"We're in the middle of war. There's no time for your filth."

He cants his head. "Very well." But he's still got that smirk on his kissable mouth.

I slip my hand into his and immediately, energy ignites between us and the air glitters like oil on water, crackling in our wake.

"Focus on what your mother feels like," Wrath instructs.

I close my eyes and focus on her.

My mom is the realest thing about me, I'm realizing. Even if I do embrace the fact that I might be a reincarnated goddess, my mother still carried me for nine months, she still gave birth to me.

She is as much a part of me as the power is now.

Sunny Low, with her boundless energy, her unflinching

belief in the good in all things, her love of Earl Grey and patchouli, her love of chasing adventure.

When I find her, her presence glows for me almost like a beacon.

I smile, giddy, and look over at Wrath. There's a new emotion in his gaze, one that I haven't seen before and I would almost swear to the gods was veneration.

"You've found her," he says. Not a question.

"Yes."

"Slide into the driver's seat, *dieva*, and carry us to her."

With his hand firmly in mine, I pull the power to me and let it transport us.

We reappear in a windowless room surrounded by gray walls with a concrete floor beneath us. It is decidedly governmental in its lack of taste.

Chaos is there with Sirene and Naomi, General Briggs too. I spot Harper's dad in the background with several other men in suits.

There are TV monitors bolted to the wall displaying several aerial feeds of the battlefield and the destruction that was wrought.

Our arrival causes the room to go quiet.

We must pose a striking contrast, Wrath and I covered in blood, them in their spotless designer suits.

These are the people behind the scenes pulling the strings while everyone else dies for their cause.

It makes me wonder about all of the chaos in our world and whether or not it can be attributed entirely to Chaos himself. Humans have their own free will and they've pissed all over this world. And now they want to piss all over Wrath's too.

"You've clearly lost," I tell them. "Now give me my mother."

Chaos comes around a table set up in the center of the room. He is unassuming in his cardigan and glasses. "Perhaps there is more to discuss, dear brother, just you and me."

Wrath shifts, his leather armor groaning.

I wanted to think Chaos was the better half the first time I met him. I wanted to like him.

Now I want to destroy him.

And I can feel Wrath's desire for the same thrumming through our renewed connection.

We've never talked about how Wrath felt about his brother, but I can sense it now. There is an overwhelming desire to make him pay for what he's done, but beneath that is a deep-seated sorrow.

It's his brother and Wrath doesn't want to murder him.

He is a villain second, a brother first.

My heart immediately aches for him.

So I make my first promise to him, shield him from the pain, the anguish, and shoulder the burden.

I disappear and reappear behind Chaos and wrap my hand around the back of his neck.

Fire licks down my arm and bubbles the skin at the nape of Chaos's neck.

He fights me at first, tries to twist in my grip. Several of the norrow appear, summoned by Chaos I guess, but they take one look at me and immediately vaporize into a swirl of dark mist.

"Wait," Chaos says around gritted teeth as the power eats away at him. "Rain. Can we...Wrath, *brother*—"

He flails, tries to get hold of me behind him, but it's no use.

Veins of embers break open in his skin, burning him from the inside out. He finally sinks to his knees and grows frantic, swinging, lashing out in any way he can.

But it only takes seconds and all that is Chaos is nothing more than ash on the air.

And when I look across the room at Wrath, his gaze is fire and light and I hear him as if he's spoken directly in my head—*thank you.*

Together, we turn to the rest of those assembled in the room.

"I'd like my mother, please," I say.

"She won't ask nicely again," Wrath adds.

No one moves, stunned in silence, frozen in shock.

"Now!" Wrath shouts.

Suddenly everyone is moving. Two military men work on the vest Mom wears while Naomi and General Briggs stand just behind her, watching with rapt attention.

Once the bomb is removed, they stand back and Mom hurries over to me, wrapping me in a hug, blood and carnage be damned.

"Oh, baby. Are you okay?"

"I'm fine, Mom. How are you?"

"Oh, don't worry about me. They gave me tea and cookies and an old copy of Better Homes and Gardens. I was occupied easily enough."

"With a bomb strapped to your chest," I mutter.

"Well...sometimes you have to weather the storm, baby."

Wrath steps forward. The crowd shrinks back.

"Tell me, *dieva*, what will their fates be?"

I give Mom a quick squeeze and then motion for her to stand behind us. Then I take my place at Wrath's side.

"I think the president has learned not to fuck with us," I say.

"Mmmm." He crosses his arms over his chest and his armor groans again.

Naomi clutches at her stupid pearls.

"I think Harper's dad is just plain greedy and if anyone here was on the edge of pissing their pants, it's him."

"I would agree," Wrath says.

"The others...they're just caught in the game. But General Briggs..."

The older man is wearing his military uniform decorated in a rainbow of bars and medals. I think he might be the driving force behind wanting to steal Wrath's throne and infiltrate Alius. He wanted to gut the world, strip it of its jewels and resources.

I've never liked that man and I like him even less now.

"General Briggs is the biggest risk to your throne," I tell Wrath.

"Our throne," he reminds me.

Yes, our throne.

"Now hold on a minute," General Briggs says as Wrath and I close in.

Unfortunately for him, the rest of those in the room shrink away. No one wants to have his back.

The darkness kicks up around Wrath, undulating in the air. The florescent lights still buzz above us, but Wrath's power still robs the room of light.

"Wait!" Briggs yells.

The darkness shoots across the room.

The sharp edge of it sinks into Briggs's chest with a heavy, wet thunk.

The man's eyes go big and blood sputters from his mouth as he tips forward and slams into the table, sending it crashing to the floor.

A coffee cup spills, then wobbles on its side before finally spinning to a stop.

No one moves.

The room is silent.

Wrath steps forward.

I swear, if the people left in the room could melt into a puddle and disappear through a crack in the floor, they would.

"You will always be inferior to me," he tells them. "I don't know how many times you need to force me to prove it to you."

He pauses and then looks at Naomi.

"If you lead this country, you need to make a decision right now—do you want peace or do you want me to destroy everything you love?"

The pearls disappear in the grip of her hand as she sucks in a deep breath. "You can't blame us for defending our country and—"

"And what of invading mine?"

Naomi clamps her mouth shut.

"Make a decision, Ms. Wright. I suggest you make the right one."

She licks her lips, lets the pearls drop against the base of her throat. The president comes back, the authority resounding in her voice as she says, "Let's consider this a truce then."

"Yes, let's. But if you threaten Rain's mother ever again or force my hand, I will strangle you with those fucking pearls and watch the life drain from your eyes."

Goosebumps travel down my arms at the threat. I know Naomi Wright is one of the smartest women around. She must know she doesn't stand a chance at this point. She's just gotta play the game whether she likes it or not.

"I understand," she says.

"Good." Wrath turns back to me. "I believe we're done here?"

"I think so." I take Mom's hand in mine. "Hold on tight."

"Why? What are you—" Before she can finish the question, we're gone.

CHAPTER
TWENTY-SIX

WE POP BACK UP AT AN ESTATE HOUSE THAT FEELS DISTINCTLY European and old. I had let Wrath guide us so I'm not familiar with the place.

Rhys is there in front of us, a glass of something dark in his hand. Emery is wiping blood from his face with a wet rag, fussing over him.

Dane and Kat are leaned against a bar, elbows on the top, drinks in hand.

"Oh good! You found your mom!" Emery comes over. I didn't see her on the battlefield and there's no blood on her, so I'm assuming she wasn't at the fight. Her hair is wound up in a messy bun. "It's a pleasure to meet you, Sunny." Emery holds out her hand before realizing there's blood on it and pulls it back.

"You are adorable," Mom says. "You remind me of a green witch I met in rural Virginia once. Any relations there?"

Emery smiles. "I don't think so, no. I'm a demon."

"Oh? Oh! That's the most interesting thing I've heard today. Do you know I used to keep a journal of the most interesting things I heard? You should try it."

Emery smiles. "Maybe I will. I like that idea."

Wrath bends down so he can speak quietly at my ear. "I need to speak with Rhys a moment. Will you be all right?"

"Of course."

He gives me a nod and then motions for Rhys to follow him out.

"This place is magnificent." Mom crosses the room, but her gaze is on the domed ceiling and the mural that covers it. There are cherubic angels and mighty gods and mythical monsters all done in the soft jewel tones reminiscent of 18th century renaissance art.

"Here." Kat hands me a glass of what smells like bourbon. "Figured you could use it."

"You have no idea," I tell her, but leave out the part about not being able to get much of a buzz anymore. Or can I? Honestly, I don't know what this new power situation is, but I'm certainly willing to give a buzz the old college try.

I follow Mom to the end of the room where she marvels at a painting of a gray-haired god carrying a torch. "If I was an interior photographer," she says, "I'd be itching for my camera."

"It is pretty magnificent."

She spins, taking in as much as she can.

"Mom."

"Hmmm?"

"I have to tell you something."

She looks at me over her shoulder. Her hair is half tied back with an elastic, but several wispy strands flutter around her face.

"I sorta married Wrath."

"Ahhh!" Mom claps her hands. "Congratulations! Does that make you a queen? I guess you did reign after all."

"I don't know the particulars yet. But listen..."

"What is it, baby?"

"I'm leaving to go with him. I think. I mean, I assume he'll want to return to his home to lord over his land and sit in his throne looking ridiculously hot and all and—"

"It'll be your life's greatest adventure," she says and takes my hand in hers, squeezes, then pats at my knuckles. "You'll remember this for the rest of your life."

Of that I have no doubt.

"I was wondering...do you want to come with?"

"To the Demon King's world?" The line of her brow rises in an arch.

"Yeah. Think about it," I say. "New land to photograph, new mountains and cliffs and oceans and waterfalls. An entire world of brand-new sights to document."

"I don't want to cramp your style."

"You won't."

"Well...it does sound like fun." She trails off in a laugh. "Who knows, maybe I'll be the first photographer to document another world for ours."

"See, yes! That could be amazing."

"But...Jeffrey..."

"Oh. What about him?"

She smiles to herself, then presses her hand to her mouth as if to hide it.

"Could he come with too?"

"Oh? I mean...I would think so? I'd have to ask, but I'd love to have him there."

"Okay. Sure. What the hell! I'd love to come with you, baby." Mom reaches over and gives me a half hug, her arm tight around my neck. "I've missed you. It'll be nice to spend some time with you."

"I agree."

I may have pretended I didn't need my mother for most of my life, but the thought of having her by my side when we literally cross over to another world...well, it makes me feel a whole lot better.

I'm realizing that I have always needed my mom—I was just too stubborn to ask for her help.

I won't make that mistake ever again.

EMERY SHOWS Mom and me to spare bedrooms in the giant manor house. Wrath's castle is officially out of the question, so Rhys apparently agreed to house us in the meantime, and I learn that it's the giant manor house on the cliff on the edge of Last Vale.

Mom decides to take a shower and lie down. I clean up in my attached bath and then head back downstairs. I find Kat and Dane in the kitchen and the second I step inside, my stomach growls.

Dane looks at my mid-section. "Are you about to give birth to a demon?"

"What? No. That's my stomach. I haven't eaten in a while."

"Goddesses eat?" Dane asks.

"Who told you I'm a goddess?"

"It's like literally everywhere," he says and rolls his eyes, then snaps his fingers. "Keep up, Rain."

Kat whacks him on the arm. I wonder how many times a day that happens? Probably more than one can count.

"I could eat," I say.

"I'll make you waffles, poppet. I make the very best around."

I look at Kat. She shrugs. "Say what you will about the prick, but he is an excellent cook for being a vampire."

Dane already has the ingredients out and a bowl for mixing.

"Can vampires eat human food?" I ask.

"Unfortunately, no. But I can smell it while it cooks and that's close enough for me."

When Emery returns, Dane hands her a plate too and we all sit at the banquet table nestled in an alcove at the back of the kitchen. Large, mullioned windows overlook the ocean though it's still too dark to see it.

By the time Rhys and Wrath come back, Emery and I are deep into our stacks of waffles while Dane recounts a hilarious story of how he once snapped Rhys's neck and then dragged the poor guy into a hospital and told the staff he was dead.

"You should have seen their faces when he came back to life!" Dane says.

"How pissed off was he?" I ask.

"Very," Rhys answers as he enters the room.

Wrath pulls out the chair next to me and sits, his body turned toward mine.

"Is everything all right?" I ask him.

"Yes. I asked Rhys if he wanted to return to Alius with us."

Emery shifts her gaze to her vampire husband. "And what did you say?"

"I said I needed to speak to you about it first."

"That's the right answer."

"Yes, little lamb, I know it was." He leans over and kisses her cheek and Emery beams.

We spend the next hour eating and drinking and I come to realize waffles and bourbon make an excellent pairing. When we're done, I'm pleasantly surprised to feel just the slightest bit of a buzz, though it took me nearly an entire bottle of bourbon to get there.

"I should probably go take a shower," I say. "I'm still grimy with war."

Wrath has been mostly silent while we hung out, but now he stands and holds out his hand for me. "Come."

I can feel the others watching us. What must they think? Not that long ago the Demon King was a ruthless, scary as hell villain.

Now he's...

Mine.

I slip my hand into his. He looks at the others. "We'll prepare this week and leave after. If you'd like to come, I'd like to have you. I need more people I can trust.

"And in my world, you can be exactly who you are. You don't have to hide it."

Dane leans back in his chair. "I have to admit, that does sound awfully enticing."

"The decision is yours to make," Wrath adds. "If you decide to come, be ready by week's end."

He doesn't wait for a response.

When we reappear in the room Rhys has given us, I look up at Wrath. "End of the week? I thought we'd at least have a few days of rest."

"I've left my throne unattended long enough." He strips out of his shirt. It's still covered in blood and gore. I try not to look too closely at it.

Just thinking about going to another world with the Demon King has my heart racing.

"Don't be nervous, *dieva*," he says, hearing the panic in my chest. "I'll be by your side."

"Easy for you to say. It's your school and you're the cool kid." I tear off my shirt and toss it in the wastebasket.

The room is all European elegance with ornate furniture and plush rugs and artwork hung in gilded frames.

I don't hate it.

"You're a reincarnated goddess," he counters. "You are the literal vision of cool kid."

202

I snort, then laugh. Hearing the Demon King refer to me as the cool kid gives me a sick sort of giddy satisfaction.

"Do you really believe that?" I ask.

He undoes his belt, yanks it out of the belt loops, and the leather snaps. "You took the last of the triad from me without even thinking about it. Yes, I very much do."

I lick my lips as he comes closer. "Isn't it a little insane to believe in some ancient myth from your world?"

"No. I think the definition of insanity is loving you. Yet here I am."

"You're an asshole."

"There she is." He closes the distance between us and takes my hair, winding it around his fist. "But just because you're a goddess doesn't mean I won't make you bow at my feet."

"Just because you're a god doesn't mean I'll do it."

He tightens his hold on my hair and a sting of pain radiates over my scalp. A goddess and yet I can still feel things. That's good because if I couldn't feel pleasure? I would riot in this bitch.

I grab Wrath around the wrist and power surges to my grip. His skin blisters immediately and he pulls back, eyes flaring red.

"You'll pay for that one, *dieva*."

"You have to catch me first." Laughing, I disappear and pop up at White Sands National Park.

I'm in only my pants and bra and goosebumps lift on my skin.

Will he find me here? Will he know how to find me?

The air snaps and I whirl just in time for Wrath to grab me in the wide span of his arms. The darkness spins around us. And threaded throughout are filaments of golden light.

"Bow to me," he says.

I sink to my knees in the sand. This isn't about submission so much as it is about trust.

We'll continue to fight each other. I think he likes it as much as I do. But I want him to know that he can trust me. And that I have faith in who we are.

The light burns brighter and the darkness writhes.

I look up at Wrath, his eyes glowing red and then he sinks to his knees in front of me.

"If you bow to me, *dieva*," he says, "then I will bow to you. My queen. Forever and an eternity." And then he threads his fingers through my hair and kisses me.

CHAPTER
TWENTY-SEVEN

THERE IS NOTHING LIKE SLEEPING IN THE DEMON KING'S ARMS AFTER he fucked me senseless, and when I wake up the next day bathed in late morning light, I marvel at how far I've come and *who* I've become.

Wrath has his arm around me, his large body spooning mine. We're both naked after fucking in the desert and showering when we returned to the house.

I am happy beyond words. And full in a way I've never been before.

"Your feet are freezing, *dieva*." His voice rumbles at the back of my neck, sending a shiver down my spine.

"Then warm me up." Neither of us misses the suggestive tone of my voice and I feel a very distinct hardness pressing into my ass.

"You wore me out last night," he says, playing a game with me. "I'm not sure I have anything left to give."

I roll to face him. His eyes are still closed, long lashes fanning over his pale cheeks. He's rumpled in the sexiest way ever. I just want to stay in this bed with him forever, screw the real world, screw his throne.

But I know the man that wears the crown would wither and die without something to rule.

And me? I'm ready for something else and I'm not so sure this world can offer me the same thing Alius can with the Demon King by my side.

I'm so ready for this adventure.

"Should we get up and have some coffee?"

He groans.

"Wait...I just had a horrible thought. Do you have coffee in Alius?"

Still grumpy, he says, "Yes."

"What about ice cream?"

"Yes."

"Wine?"

"Yes, *dieva*."

"What about *Great British Bake Off*?"

His eyes finally open, pupils shrinking in the light. "I don't know what that is so I'm assuming no."

"Wait. You don't know the absolute gold of *The Great British Bake-Off*?"

He groans. "Judging by your excitement, I will assume I don't want to."

"We need to change that."

He groans and rolls to his back. I quickly scramble over top of him, settling myself over his cock. I'm still leaking cum from last night and I slide over his length easily, the head of his shaft throbbing at my clit.

I pretend that doesn't send a thrill to my core and fireworks across my belly.

"As a goddess, I wonder if I can manifest *The Great British Bake-Off* in Alius."

"What is this bake-off anyway?"

"Oh, you'll love it."

"I doubt it."

"It's an adorable, cozy baking show where contestants all gather in a tent in the British countryside and bake pastries and pies and fuss over sponges."

"It sounds insufferable."

I rock against him, punishing him for the *very* audacity.

He groans, fingers pressing harder on my hips, guiding me over him. All of the muscle in his body tenses up as he grows harder.

"Promise me you'll watch it with me."

"No."

I slip my hand between us and take him in my grip. He's already soaked from my pussy so stroking him is easy. "Promise me."

His eyes slip closed. "Fine."

"That's what I thought."

With a growl, he takes hold of me and rolls us over so he's on top. "I should punish you for your insolence."

I boop his nose. "We both know I'll like it."

Without warning, he flips me onto my stomach, kicks my legs apart and covers my body with his. The head of his cock nestles between my legs. His hand wraps around my throat, forcing my head back.

All of the levity is gone. Now I'm the one groaning.

"Never do that again."

"Yes, daddy."

He rams into me and I let out a little yelp.

"I'm not sure if sharing cosmic power with you is a gift or a curse." He's holding himself steady, filling me up, but robbing me of the rhythm of his cock inside of me.

"Clearly, it's a gift," I say, a little breathless.

He pulls out slowly, then slides back in and I whimper.

"That's what I thought, *dieva*."

Grip tight on my throat, he picks up the pace, hitting so deep inside of me, it almost hurts.

"My queen will learn to do as I say."

"Oh, she will, will she?"

He stops again and I wiggle beneath him, pushing my ass back. Slipping his other hand around my hip, he cups me, forcing me still.

"She will."

How the hell do I say no when he's like this? I can't. I won't. He knows it. I'll push his buttons all day, every day—*outside of the bedroom.*

But here, beneath him, I'm just a girl craving the Demon King's brutal love.

"Fuck me," I beg.

"Try that again."

"Fuck me, my king."

"Good girl."

And then he slams back into me and loves me the way only a villain can, roughly and without restraint.

EPILOGUE

A WEEK LATER, I TURN A CIRCLE IN MY CONDO. THE MESS HAS BEEN cleaned up from when Ryder and his men tortured me for information on Wrath. I had to toss my TV and some of my furniture. Just as well, I suppose. Wrath warned me that I can only bring a limited number of belongings through the portal to Alius.

It's not like we're going to carry a couch through the gate.

I have two bags packed. Wrath promised me I would have the pick of whatever clothing I wanted on the other side, that money was no object. It's hard to wrap my head around it all.

In quiet moments, especially now when I'm surrounded by my belongings and the smudges of my old life, I still feel like a girl just trying to get by the best way she knew how.

Gus comes up behind me and drapes his arm over my shoulders. "We'll take care of the rest," he tells me. "We'll get it cleaned out and listed."

"Thanks, Gus. Keep whatever money you make off of it."

"Babes—"

"I insist. Put it toward your wedding. I'll be back for it once you decide on a date."

209

"Can you get emails in another dimension? Save-the-dates? Wedding invitations?"

"That's an excellent question and I'm guessing no." I wind my arm around his waist. "I'll come back to check in. So decide on a date sooner rather than later."

"We're discussing it over dinner next week. I think we'll be able to narrow it down."

"Fabulous." I turn into him and give him a hug. "This part is going to suck."

"Which part is that?"

"Saying goodbye."

He rubs his hand up and down my back. "We'll still see each other."

"Come with me."

He laughs. "I'm embarking on a new chapter in my life by getting married. I need to do that first in the world I know and understand before I throw in a world of witches and demons and vampires."

Rolling my eyes, I heave out a big sigh. "Fine."

"Maybe someday you can bring us over for a visit."

"I'd like that."

On the other end of the connection, I can feel the Demon King calling for me.

"Time to go," I say.

Gus squeezes me hard and then lifts me off my feet, whirling me around in a circle. "I'll miss you, babes."

"Miss you too." When he puts me back down, I reach up on my tiptoes to plant a kiss on his cheek. "Behave while I'm gone."

"Never."

I pull away and scoop up my two bags. I guess this is it.

I give my condo one more look. I'll miss this place, but I'm going to live in a palace. I really can't complain.

"Love you," I tell Gus.

"Love you too."

I give him a wink and then I'm gone.

WHEN I REAPPEAR, focusing on Wrath instead of a specific location, I pop up in a subterranean chamber below Last Vale.

There's another stone gate in front of us, this one newly constructed in the last week by several demons and vampires that work for Rhys.

"I said to pack light," Wrath chides.

"You saw my condo. This is light."

Rhys, Emery, Kat and Dane are there, as are Mom and Jeffrey. When Mom pitched him the idea of sculpting new work for another world, he was all too ready for the adventure. I'm so glad they're together, and that they have each other.

"Are you ready?" Wrath asks Kat.

"I think so."

"You guys really aren't coming with?" I ask.

Emery comes over to give me a hug. "Not yet. But we will."

"I want to reestablish Last Vale first," Rhys explains. "We need the city's border secure and the gate protected so that you, and we, can come and go as we please someday."

That will make it much easier to return to see Gus. I don't hate this plan.

"I'm going to need familiar faces," I tell them. "So I hope that happens sooner rather than later."

"We'll do our best," Rhys promises.

Kat steps up to the gate. "This should be interesting," she says. "Considering I've never opened a portal between worlds."

"Once you've done it, it'll be easy to do again," Wrath tells her.

"I hope that's true. Which one of you wants to bleed for the magic?"

"I will," I offer.

"Give me your hand."

I hold mine out to her and she pulls a dagger from a sheath at her waist, then drags the blade over my palm. And nothing happens.

Kat frowns, tries again.

"That might be my fault," I say and gesture for her to hand over the dagger.

The longer I'm a goddess, the harder it is to wound me, I think.

I turn the blade on myself and drag the sharp edge over the meaty part of my palm. I feel no pain, but the skin opens up and blood wells up. When I want something to happen, it will. It's as easy as that.

Kat takes the dagger back and wipes it off on her dark jeans, then resheaths it. "To the doorway with you."

I step up the three steps to the stone doorway and Wrath comes to stand beside me. Mom and Jeffrey are behind us. Wrath says to them, "Follow us through immediately. Do not hesitate."

"Of course," Jeffrey says and takes Mom's hand in his.

Wrath turns to me. "You ready, *dieva*?"

Through the connection, his hope radiates back to me.

"I'm ready."

I place my bloody palm to the stone and behind us, Kat calls out a string of foreign words.

The stone melts away and light shines through from the other side.

It's impossible to make out what lays beyond.

A little sliver of fear jams into my heart, but Wrath takes my hand in his. His is warm, solid, and real.

"Whatever we do," he tells me, "we do it together. I will be by your side."

I take a deep breath and nod.

"You take the first step, *dieva*," he says, "and I will follow."

I look back and Rhys and Kat and Emery and Dane wave goodbye.

And I take the first step into a new world with the Demon King by my side, now his queen.

And I will Reign.

I CAN'T BELIEVE THE TRILOGY IS FINISHED! This was such a joy to write. I loved Wrath and Rain and every single time they were on the page, it was a delight.

If you want to spend just a little more time with the characters, how about a bonus scene?

Rain finally talks Wrath into watching *Great British Bake Off* and then they take a break for *other things*.

Sign-up here:
https://www.subscribepage.com/nikkistcrowebonus

Also by Nikki St. Crowe

Vicious Lost Boys

The Never King

The Dark One

Their Vicious Darling

The Fae Princes

Wrath & Rain Trilogy

Ruthless Demon King

Sinful Demon King

Vengeful Demon King

Wrath & Reign Omnibus

House Roman

A Dark Vampire Curse

Midnight Harbor

Hot Vampire Next Door (ongoing Vella serial)

Hot Vampire Next Door: Season One (ebook)

Hot Vampire Next Door: Season Two (ebook)

Hot Vampire Next Door: Season Three (ebook)

Hot Vampire Next Door: Season Four (ebook)

Bonus Scene Anthology

Ink & Feathers

About the Author

Nikki St. Crowe has been writing for as long as she can remember. Her first book, written in the 4th grade, was about a magical mansion full of treasure. While she still loves writing about magic, she's ditched the treasure for something better: villains, monsters, and anti-heroes, and the women who make them wild.

These days, when Nikki isn't writing or daydreaming about villains, she can either be found in the woods or at home with her husband and daughter.

Newsletter Sign-Up
www.subscribepage.com/nikkistcrowe

Follow Nikki on Instagram
www.instagram.com/nikkistcrowe

Join Nikki's Facebook Group
www.facebook.com/groups/nikkistcrowesnest

Visit Nikki on the web at:
www.nikkistcrowe.com

instagram.com/nikkistcrowe

tiktok.com/@nikkistcrowe

facebook.com/authornikkistcrowe

amazon.com/Nikki-St-Crowe/e/B098PJW25Y

bookbub.com/profile/nikki-st-crowe